"We got married for such...silly reasons."

Belle's tone was hostile as she remembered the pain of her all-too-brief marriage to Nick.

"Silly, but not shameful," Nick replied. He lifted his left hand and looked thoughtfuly at his wedding ring. "Now, this little item has come in useful.... It's prevented one or two women from asking for more than I can give."

"You are appalling," she said with a sort of resignation. He was so flawed, so empty...and so inexpressibly dear to her.

"Does your ring still fit?" he asked abruptly, picking up her left hand in his.

"No, Nick, don't," she protested as he slipped the familiar ring back on her finger, the ring she'd left behind the night she'd walked out on him.

He raised her hand to his lips, and when his tongue gently touched the smooth flesh, she felt the old familiar melting sensation begin. It wasn't fair, she thought wildly, that he should be the only man who could make her feel like this.

JAYNE BAULING wrote for years before she found the confidence to let anyone see what she was doing. Now she writes full-time. But she still finds time to putter in her large untidy garden and breed sealpoint cats. Traveling, she says, is her obsession—so for her, real-life romance is often necessarily a long-distance affair.

Books by Jayne Bauling

HARLEQUIN PRESENTS

247—WALK IN THE SHADOWS
505—WAIT FOR THE STORM
663—VALENTINE'S DAY
775—RAGE TO POSSESS
863—MATCHING PAIR
879—THAI TRIANGLE

These books may be available at your local bookseller.

JAYNE BAULING

to fill a silence

Harlequin Books

TORONTO • NEW YORK • LONDON
AMSTERDAM • PARIS • SYDNEY • HAMBURG
STOCKHOLM • ATHENS • TOKYO • MILAN

Harlequin Presents first edition September 1986
ISBN 0-373-10911-3

Original hardcover edition published in 1985
by Mills & Boon Limited

CHAPTER ONE

'YOUR hair! You've cut it.' The words were accusing.

This was unfair, Belle thought wildly, forced to stand like a statue just inside the lounge door because her legs were suddenly incapable of carrying her any further. It was unfair because she had had no warning. He was the last person she would have expected to find here in the lounge of the large apartment she shared with three other people, whereas he was unsurprised by her arrival. She knew him well enough to be sure of that.

She would have lost her colour, had she not been pale already. It had been a difficult, frustrating day, and the short walk home from her tiny, hot office had sapped the last of her energy because Taipei in mid-summer was intolerably humid, set in a basin as it was, surrounded by mountains on all sides. She had walked slowly, her head and shoulders bent under the oppressive heat, and she had nearly been run over twice, once by a bus and then by one of the thousands of small motorbikes that made traffic one of Taiwan's most serious problems, this particular one almost invisible beneath the family it bore, small daughter sandwiched between her parents while a long basket had been attached to the front to accommodate a baby of not older than six months.

Such encounters still unnerved her after all this time, and the heat had done nothing to improve her mood. Her thin cotton top of palest sage-green, worn belted over a matching skirt, was sticking to her back between her shoulder blades, and she knew her make-up had probably melted away during the short walk home.

Resentment tightened her passionate mouth. She had been looking forward to reaching the air-conditioned spaciousness of the apartment. She had to return to her office later to file a report to the Canadian radio network, one of her newest clients, but she had promised herself a drink, a shower and, possibly, solitude in which to enjoy a leisurely supper if she felt hungry, as she and the others seldom encountered each other, none of their jobs involving regular hours.

Now here they all were, grouped around Nick as if he were some sort of guru, which in media terms he was, she supposed reluctantly, and Marilyn had obviously made some sort of effort to conceal the chaos that normally characterised the haphazardly furnished lounge, because their assorted typewriters and notes were no longer strewn all over the carpet, chairs and coffee table, but were confined to the two desks against the inside wall, while a week's collection of glasses and cups had disappeared and the ashtrays were empty.

Swallowing painfully and gripping the strap of her soft leather bag so tightly that her knuckles showed white, Belle looked at Nick again. He was smiling at her, damn him, the same to-hell-with-the-world smile that had always captivated her—smiling because it didn't matter to him that they were meeting like this after five years. It meant nothing to him; he hadn't been hurt.

Damn him, she thought again, dropping her bag and forcing her legs to carry her further into the room, wearing as casual a smile as she could manage because it was the only way to cope.

'Hullo, Nick,' she said easily.

The other three were looking startled. 'Have you by any chance been holding out on us, Belle?' Terry Whelan demanded.

'You never told us you knew Nick Rosney,' Travis Schallau agreed, his hazel eyes noting the little things that gave her away.

'Oh, she never really knew me, Schallau,' Nick laughed. 'She merely married me.'

Belle flinched visibly. The remark was vintage Nick Rosney. A born iconoclast, he always said what was better left unspoken, and he always created a sensation. She shouldn't be surprised, or hurt. It wasn't as if he were doing it deliberately, trying to distress her. To Nick, it undoubtedly seemed quite genuinely amusing, the fact that once, on an impulse, he had got married. It probably made a good story, because he would be able to tell it without bitterness. His impulse hadn't even cost him very much financially, since she had refused to accept the allowance he had wanted to make her.

His words had definitely created a sensation. The other three were staring at her as if they had never seen her before.

'Hell!' Travis shook his head. 'When was this, Belle?'

'All of five and a half years ago,' Nick answered for her.

'And all of five years ago we parted,' Belle supplied tartly, not wanting to give him the satisfaction of thinking his presence had rendered her speechless.

Nick nodded. 'We're divorced,' he added with a faint smile, and Belle could have hit him. He didn't have to make quite such a comedy of it. It hadn't been funny at the time; not for her, anyway. It had hurt.

The others were evidently having difficulty in

assimilating these revelations about someone they had
lived with for the past year.

'Hell! When I told you about my own marriage and
divorce, you never said a word about yours,' Travis
reproached her.

'Who boasts about the mistakes of their youth?'
Belle retorted with a stinging smile for Nick, who
merely laughed. 'Yours was mature folly, Travis.'

'Yeah, you can only have been a baby five years
ago,' Travis realised, and then gave Nick an apologetic
glance.

'But your name is Tyler,' Marilyn McMillan
protested.

'Yes, I'm interested to know why you reverted to
your maiden name, Belle?' Nick questioned smoothly.
'You were perfectly entitled to call yourself Rosney.'

'I didn't think there was room for two Rosneys in
the media,' she responded smartly. 'I might have been
accused of capitalising on your name.'

'Ah!' His smile was sardonic. 'So what were you
really doing? Trying to compete with me?'

'I'm not that conceited, Nick, and I've kept out of
television, in case you didn't know.' Belle sank into a
chair close to his.

'All the same, you've branched out in an unexpected
direction,' he commented, watching her face. 'Five
years ago, in London, I couldn't have seen you
freelancing as a stringer.'

'As Travis mentioned, I was a baby then.
Actually, it was something you said, Nick. You said
good media people didn't sit in air-conditioned
offices getting news through a telephone; they went
out and got the winds of the world in their faces. I
haven't been in the hot spots of the globe like you,
but in my way, I've tried.' With a sigh, she eased
off her soft leather sandals. 'And sometimes, like

today, I wonder why. Won't someone please get me a drink?'

'Tough day, baby?' Travis stood up.

'I've had Government giving me uphill about my use of the name Taiwan in reports again,' she explained. 'I suggested I could revert to Formosa, but that didn't please them. Republic of China is the only thing that will satisfy them, never mind that my clients don't like it because half their readers and listeners think I'm referring to mainland China.'

'Yes, I tried to ring you to say Nick would be coming round and wanted to see us all, and little Suzie Wong told me in hushed tones that you were tied up,' Terry recalled.

'I wish you'd stop calling her that, Terry,' Belle said absently, taking the drink Travis had mixed for her and looking at her ex-husband. 'What's it all about, Nick? Is something brewing? I'd have said we were comparatively peaceful just now, though never secure, but I'm the first to admit that I lack your sixth sense.'

It was the difference between the great and the merely good, she knew, that instinct for news, and Nick was an acknowledged genius. That was why her three friends were still looking as awed as she had once felt on meeting him. None of them was British, but Nick Rosney was as famous in otheir countries as he was at home. Presidents respected him; task forces gave him accreditation—and only she knew that he was fatally flawed, incapable of bringing any real emotion to his personal life because all that went into Nick Rosney was given to his work which, in the best media tradition, could be said to consist of comforting the afflicted and afflicting the comfortable.

He shook his dark head, smiling at her. 'This is in the nature of a holiday for me, Belle. I'm doing a short series on the phenomenon of pariah nations, the polecats of the world. It interests me and they have many features in common, quite apart from necessity driving them into each other's arms. For instance, most of them have developed very vigorous economies. I've just come from filming in South Korea, and after Taiwan ... Well, Israel and South Africa are possibilities, but I may have to leave them to my assistant, depending on what develops where. The point is, I've never spent long in Taiwan, so I need the help of those who know it better than I. It was your name I was given in London, coincidence being a mischievous thing. You've been here a year now, haven't you?'

'And as we've already said, if there's anything the rest of us can do, tell you or show you, you have only to ask,' Travis said. 'But what's the basic idea?'

As they talked, Belle watched Nick with an old pain reawakened. It had never really gone away; it had merely been suppressed, and she had always been aware of it. She may have been naïve and stupid once, but in some things she knew herself well and there were truths that could never be denied.

She had no need to look for changes in him. She had seen him on television too often down the years to be shocked or surprised by the marks of time and, anyway, they were few. He was leaner and harder, she thought, and the laughter grooves at either side of his mouth were no longer the only lines on the handsome tanned face, but considering that he was now thirty-four, ten years older than her, he had been remarkably fortunate. When she thought of the wars he had covered, and some of the dangers he had faced, his arrest and incarceration in a South American country two years ago for instance, she shuddered and wondered how he could still laugh. Only, he never had laughed at those things. It was only the personal that he was incapable of taking seriously, perhaps because a broken relationship seemed trivial when set beside the horrors and mass suffering he and his team covered.

She had probably changed more than he had. From eighteen to twenty-four was a longer journey than from twenty-eight to thirty-four. It was a time for growing and getting to know yourself, your range and your limitations. She was no longer the self-deluding girl she had been when they had met, while Nick was still—Nick, only more so. The black hair that was blue-black in some lights still fell down in a curve over his intelligent brow, and she still thought his eyes were the bluest she had ever seen, a deep, dark colour gleaming and sparkling between incredibly long eyelashes. There was the smiling, beautiful mouth that had once travelled the length of her body, the aquiline nose, the perfect bone-structure perhaps even more fleshless than it had been and therefore more arresting, the deep golden tan, the long tapering hands that had caressed her with so much skill and such indifference . . .

That had been where the true cruelty lay, not in cruelty itself or in abuse, but in his indifference.

He was wearing a blue shirt and faded jeans that fitted close against his lean hips and long thighs. Belle felt the sharp, powerful tug of desire as she looked at him, just as she had so many years ago on first meeting him in the flesh, but now she could suppress it. She wasn't getting caught up in that syndrome again. Thank God she was no longer eighteen; she was unlikely to make a fool of herself a second time— because it had to be admitted: she had no one but herself to blame for the nights she had spent crying for Nick. He had never lied to her, he had never pretended to love her, but she, with the monumental conceit of her youth, had deluded herself into believing that he did so. She had even been arrogant enough to think she understood him, when there was really nothing there to understand because Nick Rosney, the private man, was merely a hollow shell.

Now she knew the truth and recognised the futility of it all, and yet she could still mourn for her marriage and feel shame for her failure to prevent its swift disintegration. It had all been so pathetic, really. It wasn't even as if anyone had come between them. Quite simply, their marriage had broken down—irretrievably.

It had been a crazy thing to do, anyway, marrying the way they had, and even crazier on Nick's part than on hers because he had done it on a whim, simply because he had been in the mood to marry. She at least had had the excuse of being in love with him.

She hadn't really been paying attention to what was being said, so when Nick turned his head and looked at her enquiringly, she stared back at him blankly.

'What about it, Belle?' he asked with his charming, meaningless smile. 'Can I rely on you for information, have access to any notes you may have compiled, etcetera?'

'Nick . . .' Belle felt trapped. She didn't want anything to do with him. She didn't want to have to see him again.

'For old time's sake.' That smile really was quite dazzling.

She looked at the others, knowing they admired Nick's attitude to the fact that they had once been married. They probably thought it civilised and would expect her to take a similar line, as would Nick because, to be fair to him, it simply wouldn't have occurred to him that their reunion might have occasioned her pain and distress.

Travis, Terry and Marilyn were looking at her expectantly. Belle swallowed the rest of her drink and returned Nick's smile with a brilliant one of her own. She still had her pride.

'Of course, Nick,' she assured him brightly. 'For old time's sake . . . We might even find the time to catch up on all each other's news.'

'Let's hope so.' He looked at the others and then at her again. 'My team are having a party at the hotel tonight so you could come along and meet them if you're free, all of you. Come in an hour or so, or when you can. It's the Ambassador. Just ask for my suite.'

The others were making sounds of acceptance, but Belle smiled with spurious regret. 'Unfortunately I can't make it. I have to return to my office and make a report for my Canadian clients. They're particular about the times I file.'

'Well, come when you're through,' Nick said easily. 'It shouldn't take you long. In fact, I'll come with you and we can go on to the hotel together.'

'Oh, please don't bother, Nick,' Belle demurred, wanting to scream. 'I've a few other things to do, and then, it sometimes takes me a while to get through, telephones being what they are, so I've no idea how long I'll be.'

He shrugged dismissively. 'I'm not pressed for time, tonight at any rate, and I'd like to see where you operate from, Belle.'

'Well, I must shower and change first,' she gave in with resigned impatience, afraid of protesting too much in front of the others. Why did this first meeting after long years have to take place before witnesses?

'I'll wait.'

'Have another drink,' Travis offered while Belle stood up, retrieved her shoes and bag and went to her bedroom.

She showered and put on fresh clothes with a speed that stemmed from temper, her movements quick and angry. She needed time in which to prepare herself for having Nick temporarily back in her life, and he wasn't giving it to her, but the most annoying part of it was the knowledge that he wasn't doing it deliberately. He wasn't trying to be cruel or seeking to disconcert her. Once again, he was acting purely out of indifference, unable to imagine that her emotional equilibrium might have been disturbed by his advent. As he saw it, he had emerged from their marriage unscathed, free of regrets and hang-ups, so she ought to be the same.

Sighing, Belle shook her head slightly. That was Nick. She just had to accept it and do her best not to disillusion him, because he would despise her if he guessed the emotional turmoil he had created. The memory of his derision, when she had shown any emotion during the course of their brief marriage, was still a raw wound, and she didn't think it would ever heal.

She was doing her make-up when Travis knocked at her door and entered in response to her bidding.

'Are you okay?' he wanted to know. 'It was a bit of a shock to you, wasn't it?'

Belle smiled wryly as his reflection appeared behind hers. Travis was American, the correspondent for a New York-based news magazine, and she was closer to him than to Terry or Marilyn, who were too absorbed in their private sex war to have much time for anyone else, although she always found their quarrels amusing when she wasn't pitying them. They both pretended their hostility arose out of the traditional love–hate relationship between their two countries with the Tasman dividing them, but Belle had long ago discerned the strong underlying attraction that so often manifested itself in violent antagonism.

It was funny: she and Nick had never experienced that sort of antagonism; they had got on well and liked each other from the start; but then, she could hardly be said to have attracted Nick in anything more than a lukewarm way. She had just happened to be the girl he was seeing when some mischievous imp had put it into his head to get married.

'I'll survive,' she told Travis drily, closing her *Santé* scent bottle and standing up.

'Sure you will, but not without hurting.' He looked at her kindly. 'That marriage of yours didn't touch you as lightly as it did him, did it?'

'I was the sucker,' she admitted, picking up her bag.

'What happened?'

'Nothing, really,' Belle responded ruefully, still unable to talk about it because talking brought the pain back too sharply. 'We just made a mistake; we were incompatible. Perhaps Nick's career got in the way . . . I don't know.'

'Uhuh! I guess a man like that doesn't have much left to bring to something as personal as marriage,' Travis mused, watching her. 'That's why you got hurt and he didn't. He's a genius, Belle, a different breed.'

'And that's why we have to forgive him?' She couldn't quite hide her bitterness, but then she smiled and shook her head. 'It's all right, I have actually forgiven him, if there was anything to forgive. Most of it was my fault—the failure was mine. I was too young to see clearly, and too young to handle it when I did begin to see. So I got out, and he let me, with considerable relief if the way he arranged our divorce was anything to go by.'

She didn't know how he had done it, but it had all been achieved so quickly and easily that they hadn't even needed to contact each other again. Once more, that was typical of Nick Rosney. He wasn't a man who was prepared to live with his mistakes; if he made an error, he lost no time in correcting it.

'Has this been why you've refused to let your relationship with me develop beyond friendship?' Travis asked gently.

Belle's expression grew hunted. 'Travis, I . . . Do you mean, has my one experience of the man–woman thing disenchanted me for life?'

'Well, that too. It could have made you wary, or even cynical, but I really meant . . . Are you still in love with Nick Rosney?' He saw her agitation, the way her shadowy green eyes went to the door as if she longed to escape, and his expression grew contrite. 'I'm being unfair, aren't I? As if you weren't under enough pressure already . . . Forget it, honey. We'll talk another time. He's waiting for you out there.'

'Pacing the floor?'

Belle smiled faintly. Nick had no gift for relaxation. He had never been able to sit still for long, and his mother had told her he had been hyperactive as a child. It was strange, when he was so utterly incapable of personal emotion, that he should simultaneously be the most temperamental and highly strung man she had ever known. It was a contradiction, and yet it was true of Nick.

Once, though, she had thought him capable of emotion but unable to express it. That had been her major mistake and the cause of so much suffering. She knew better now. Never again would she credit Nick with feelings he was incapable of experiencing.

'Ready? Let's go then,' he said as soon as she re-entered the lounge, his vivid eyes sweeping her fresh outfit of cream dungarees worn over a pale olive T-shirt.

For the first time since finding him here, Belle felt a little bubble of spontaneous laughter rising within her. There was no one like Nick. He was always in a hurry, always vibrant with life and energy, and somehow it was infectious. She seemed to catch some of his restless impatience, and she always felt her awareness, her perceptions, to be sharpened in his presence. She experienced things more acutely—including pain, and that was why she didn't want him back in her life. Pain was the last thing she needed. She had had her share of that.

'Do we walk or take a taxi?' he asked when they were out in the busy street.

'Either. A taxi, I think,' Belle decided. 'I've had one hot walk already today. Did you know that there are about three thousand taxis here and that whatever the length of your journey, a ride costs one hundred New Taiwan dollars? That's a little over two U.S. dollars.'

'The only difficulty I've discovered so far is that none of the drivers can speak English,' Nick laughed.

'You need to carry cards.'

'Have you learnt any Mandarin yet?'

'Not yet,' she admitted. 'But Sue-Ching, my assistant, has been trying to teach me. She says it's a much more attractive language than the Cantonese spoken in Hong Kong.'

A taxi stopped for them and Belle showed the driver the card Sue-Ching had prepared for her, giving the address of her office in the Chinese characters. As they moved off, only to become embroiled in a traffic jam half a block further on, she felt the heat of awareness stealing over her, knowing Nick was looking at her. He was the only man who could make her blush.

'Why did you do it?' he asked abruptly.

'What?' Her shadow-filled green eyes flew to his handsome face.

'Your lovely hair. Why did you cut it?'

Her hair was very dark, and radiant, with dark red glints in certain lights, and in the days of their marriage she had worn it long and straight with a deep fringe. Her stomach seemed to tighten at the memory of Nick letting its silken mass pour through his hands when they made love. Now it was cut fairly short and layered, the fringe softly feathered, the expert styling emphasising the delicate shape of her head as well as her prominent cheekbones and making her dark, changeable green eyes look larger. She hadn't liked it at first, thinking it made her look too vulnerable, but she had grown accustomed to it and no longer thought of growing it again.

'I'd hate to have long hair in this climate,' she told Nick somewhat crossly, angry with herself for remembering things that had once melted her bones.

'You promised me you'd never cut it.'

Choosing her words carefully and not quite meeting his eyes, she said slowly, 'I don't want to be rude, Nick, and I'm certainly not reproaching you for anything, but I didn't think you had the right to expect me to keep such promises after we parted.'

Initially, in fact, she had hacked at her hair herself in a fit of temper in the early hours of a dark morning when she had lain sleepless all night, tortured by the memory of all that had been sweet in their marriage, the good times that rose up to reproach her for having lacked the strength to endure the bad.

'And after we'd both broken so many more important promises,' Nick agreed with unusual seriousness. 'God, is the traffic always this bad?'

'The fact that it's summer vacation makes it worse, but it is a major problem,' she offered, grateful for an impersonal subject. 'What sort of information do you what about Taiwan? I can warn you now that wherever you go here, the people will tell you that traffic and education are the big problems, and God knows the latter is a terrifyingly competitive system and I wouldn't want any child of mine subjected to those long hours of study. But the real problem and the real tragedy is Taiwan's relations with mainland China. There are old people who came over from there and their children are always distressed when they start expressing a longing to return before they die.'

'Yes, it's virtually a natural instinct in the crazy race of human beings, the need to die in one's own country.' Nick paused. 'It suits you, actually.'

'What?' Belle was disconcerted again.

'Your hair.' He smiled at her. 'But you're too thin. You've lost a lot of weight.'

He wouldn't think she was too thin if he could have seen her in the months immediately following their parting, she thought acidly, remembering how misery, guilt and resentment had made her unable to face food of any sort. She really hadn't had much backbone in those days, and she had starved herself sick.

'Puppy fat. Honestly, Nick, you can't expect me not to have changed!' she exclaimed with a touch of asperity. 'I wouldn't be worth much as a woman if I'd stayed the same as I was five years ago, physically or mentally.'

'Oh, I don't know. I don't think I've changed much,' he claimed with the ghost of a grin.

'You were already a man five years ago. I was only eighteen, nineteen.' She hesitated. 'You married a child, Nick.'

It was the nearest she could come to an apology at that moment, but she felt she owed him that much at least. Over the years, as she had learnt to know herself, she had been shocked to look back and discover how much of the blame for their disastrous marriage must be laid at her feet. She had made so many mistakes, out of ignorance or selfishness, and she could only thank God that Nick hadn't really loved her. Had he done so, she could have hurt him appallingly with her insensitivity, but fortunately he had been just as lacking in sensitivity as far as his personal life was concerned, so at least she had the meagre solace of knowing that she had caused anguish to no one but herself. She could never have forgiven herself, had she made Nick suffer.

'Yes, a mere baby, as Schallau realised just now. It was a crazy, impetuous thing to do,' Nick admitted carelessly, laughing a little. 'And hardly fair to you. I don't know what got into me.'

And that, Belle supposed bleakly, was his apology.

She looked at him helplessly. She would never really understand him, because he was a mass of contradictions. It seemed so incredible that a man who cared so passionately about the anguish of the masses in the Lebanon, in Afghanistan, in half-a-dozen other countries, in which he had risked his life over and over again to bring news of their plight to the world, should be so emotionally sterile in his personal life. She remembered his commentary on the refugee camps in Thailand, a bitter, eloquent demand that the rest of the free world share the burden that country has assumed, and she set that against his callous attitude to their marriage. Almost, he might have had a split personality, the two men were so hard to reconcile.

He was resilient and intelligent, and yet insensitive in that one way. He was also a curiously fragile human being, and that was another paradox, because how could someone inviolable be fragile? And yet that was what Nick Rosney was; it was one of the things she had always known about him. He was too highly strung, with a volatile temperament that he tried to conceal but which occasionally betrayed him and added to his reputation for a touch of craziness. Belle still remembered the time he had snatched her *1812 Overture* off the music centre after dragging the needle across it. He had broken it and flung the pieces at her before stalking out of the room and she had wondered if she had married a schizophrenic.

It was just as well, she had sometimes thought, that, with his temperament, he was incapable of loving, because he would have touched the heights, but the inevitable depths would have been unbearable.

He even revealed that fragility in certain ways although he was probably unaware of it. His beautiful mouth, when he wasn't smiling or laughing, indicated a certain sensitivity, and there were faint shadows around his eyes because not even his resilience was truly invincible. Belle still carried the aching memory of his fatigue on his returns to England from the trouble-spots of the world, with his face all planes and angles, shadowed with weariness and disgust, so that it was a study in black, white and grey, the only colour being in his eyes, because true, deep tiredness had even blanched his permanent tan. All he had wanted to do on those occasions was to hold her, and . . .

Belle's mind skipped away from the recollection. She had failed him so badly then, and she couldn't rid herself of a sense of guilt, even after all this time, even knowing that since he hadn't loved her, he hadn't really merited anything better of her.

She must stop remembering like this or she would give herself away, and God knew what reaction that would elicit—derision most probably, but possibly pity or embarrassment. She just didn't want to find out.

She said, in a neutral voice, 'I still haven't grasped exactly what it is you want to know about Taiwan, Nick. How can I help you?'

'Well, some of your reports on the economic situation have been excellent, but to begin with, I think I'd just like to discuss it with you in general terms, draw on your impressions so that I know what to look for and where.' Pausing, he gave her his quick scintillating smile. 'I hope you don't mind too much my coming back into your life like this? I promise you it won't be for long.'

'Why should I mind?' She sounded aggressive, because she did mind.

'Well, you shouldn't, of course,' Nick returned mildly. 'And I'm relieved if you don't. It was just that, remembering your penchant for emotional scenes, I was a bit afraid you'd be tempted to make a drama out of my presence.'

Oh, God, he really was a cruel bastard, she thought, colour stinging her normally pale cheeks as she drew her lips firmly together, because they suddenly had a tendency to tremble.

'It's not only physically that I've changed, Nick.' Her voice shook with a mixture of anger and distress. 'I've done a bit of growing in other ways too, you know.'

'Why are you sounding so hostile?' Nick's vivid eyes were brilliant slits between the long screening eyelashes.

'I'm not!' Belle heard herself with disgust. Even now, he still had the power to reduce her to this sort of childishness, damn him!

He laughed gently. 'You always did take me far too seriously, Belle.'

As if she didn't know that!

She closed her eyes for a moment. How was she

going to endure it, seeing him in the days to come? She didn't think she had the strength to bear the constant reminder of what a fool she had been—what a fool she still was, mourning the loss of something she had never really had.

Her distressed anxiety intensified as their taxi finally deposited them at their destination. Momentarily, as she stepped on to the crowded pavement, Nick's slim tapering hand closed round her upper arm, evoking a flood of memories that came accompanied by the old familiar lurch in her loins. He was still the only man whose touch could weaken her and make her both burn and shiver at the same time.

She wished he hadn't come to Taiwan, and she wished even more fervently that she had never met and married him.

CHAPTER TWO

BELLE would never have met Nick, but for the mischievous chances of fate. As a very junior staffer on a woman's magazine, she would never normally have been sent to interview him.

Inevitably they had had to feature him. He had been the man of the moment, the newsmaker of that year. Still in his twenties, he was attractive, talented and controversial. His career had followed a swift upward course and his women were not only beautiful but usually famous in their own right, highly visible people. When a series of much-publicised rows had culminated in the network moguls granting Nick Rosney complete autonomy over everything he did, plus a breathtaking salary, their editor had decided the time had come to make him man of the week. Loyal to his media colleagues, he had agreed to an interview.

They had been short-staffed at the time due to a flu epidemic, but Belle's superior had been too tough to succumb to anything so prosaic. Instead, dramatically, she had been struck down with acute appendicitis on the point of leaving to interview the famous man, but even as she was being lifted into the ambulance she had maintained enough presence of mind to delegate the task to Belle, the only staffer still available.

'And for pity's sake, don't let him seduce you,' she had concluded her instructions. 'He's notorious for it, and he's always the one who walks away laughing.'

Belle had smiled. She had read about his women and she had known she wasn't in their league. She was eighteen years old and five pounds overweight.

He had seduced her, though, but only mentally and emotionally. Physically, he had waited until they were legally married.

She had seen him on television and admired him, but encountering him in the flesh was altogether a different matter. He had been tangible, somehow reachable, a human being, just like her. Belle had looked at Nick Rosney, and loved.

The brilliant blue eyes had been hypnotic and the famous mouth had quirked with irresistible amusement as she had stood on the doorstep of his light, bright and comfortable Wimbledon home, stammering out her explanation.

'Yes,' he had murmured when she had ground to an embarrassed halt. 'Yes, I think I've got the gist of it. You've just omitted to tell me your name?'

'Belle,' she had whispered. 'Belle Tyler.'

'Belle,' he had repeated, his vivid eyes still fixed on her face, and in that moment her doom had been sealed. 'How appropriate.'

He had led her inside, given her a drink and made her laugh.

At the end of an hour they had both been laughing, delighted with each other. When he had asked her to have dinner with him that night, she had had no thought of refusal. It hadn't seemed like patronage. Somehow, they had become equals, appreciative of each other, understanding each other.

She had been that much of a fool, Belle could think five and a half years later.

They had gone out together every night for a week, always to dinner, never to any sort of entertainment because, Belle suspected, Nick was incapable of remaining silent for the length of even the shortest theatrical, balletic or operatic act. He liked to talk, and she liked to hear him. Occasionally there had been dancing to a band at the places where they dined, but although he had been willing to take her on to the dance floor, she had discovered that he was that rarest of human beings, a man who hated music. Linda Ronstadt, laid back and singing the schmaltzy old songs like *I've Got A Crush On You*, he could take, but anything faster or louder was intolerable to his ears and when she had confessed a liking for Pink Floyd, Elton John and Bob Geldof, he had grimaced before smiling tolerantly and murmuring facetiously: 'To each his own.'

When they had danced, he had talked all the time. They had always attended establishments frequented by the famous, and Nick had seemed to know them all. He had made her laugh with outrageous stories about them that would never get into print for one reason or another. He was, it seemed to her, incapable of seriousness.

But she had loved him . . .

He could have taken her to bed after their first date. She had been besotted, adoring, but already wise enough to know she mustn't reveal the truth too blatantly. Understanding of Nick had come quickly, and she had known that displays of emotion irritated him.

Only, her comprehension of him hadn't gone deep enough in those days, she could reflect now. She had been so stupidly confident, once he started taking her out. It had never occurred to her to wonder why he was doing so, when she was so far removed from the legions of other women who had passed through his life and his bed. Quite simply, she had reasoned that since he could have no ulterior motive, he must be doing it because he—liked her, at the very least.

Only now, when her understanding went deeper than a superficial awareness based on observation, could she see the truth of it. Nick had been on holiday, and consequently he was bored. It was a permanent condition in him when he wasn't working, because he was incapable of deriving satisfaction from his personal life. A born fieldman, he could only find fulfilment of any sort in the frontline.

An eighteen-year-old girl whom no one had ever heard of had been a novelty, a diversion. It had amused him to see the perplexity on the faces of the famous friends they kept meeting in restaurants, and he would introduce her with his most wicked smile and watch them trying to place her.

And she, poor fool, had thought he introduced her to them because he was proud of her!

But merely taking her out hadn't been different enough to satisfy Nick for long. For his next trick, he decided to do something really outrageous. He would marry her!

The memory of that night was branded into her brain and heart, to serve for evermore as a warning, and she would never be free of the constant reminder of her humiliating stupidity.

The setting had been a small, select restaurant, specialising in Italian food and frequented mainly by entertainment and media people. The lighting was soft and romantic, and for once Nick had been silent, staring moodily at her across the small table.

That brooding gaze had given her hope. Perhaps tonight he would abandon the chilling restraint he had exercised all week when kissing her, and would make love to her properly, thereby freeing her to respond with all the passionate love and longing she was keeping carefully locked in her heart until such time as he indicated that he was ready to accept it.

He had kissed her every night on taking her back to the flat she shared with two other girls, but always so coolly, maintaining a space between them, while his hands had never strayed from her shoulders, and it had been killing her, trying to stifle her natural need to respond, but she had dared not reveal her desire after that first time. Then, when he had kissed her, she had wound her arms about his neck, her fingers twining in his jet black hair to bring his head closer and deepen their kiss, and she had arched so that her body was pressed against him, her thighs trembling against the hardness of his. Instantly, Nick had put her away from him, quite gently, but Belle had not missed his fleeting expression of annoyance.

So, she had only been able to wait, and wonder at his reserve, because he had a reputation as a perfect lover, exciting and considerate.

Of course, it was possible that she didn't attract him sexually, but she had swiftly discarded the thought, because why else would he be taking her out? Consideration for her youth was another possibility. His previous lovers had all been older than her and presumably experienced. If that was the explanation, she was touched, but she hoped he wouldn't be patient much longer. She knew herself. She knew she loved him and she knew what she wanted. She was ready for him. He had no need to take it slowly.

Tonight, perhaps . . . The way his eyes smouldered as he had looked at her suggested a change in mood, and there was something sensual about the twist of his lips.

So she had felt almost disappointed when he had dispelled the silence with a restless laugh.

'What's funny?' she had asked gently. He found humour in most things, although his view was often cynical.

'Oh, I don't know. What is?'

'Life?' she had suggested flippantly.

'It can be. But somehow mine lacks much comedy just now.' He had moved irritably, his expression dissatisfied. 'I think I'll have to change it.'

'In what way?' she had asked.

'Oh, what the hell!' Nick had laughed again, a hard, reckless sound. 'I'm tired of being a bachelor, Belle. Let's get married.'

It had hardly been a romantic proposal, but it had knocked all the breath out of her lungs. Shocked, she had stared at him. Then a slow smile had begun in her eyes and had gradually brought a curve to her lips, and mingling with her joy had been a wry tenderness for him, an odd feeling of indulgence.

It was strange and somehow tragic that the man who was so eloquent in commenting on the ravages of war and disaster, and so mercilessly articulate and comprehensive in interrogating heads of state around the globe, should be so utterly incapable of expressing his deepest feelings.

Because she had been convinced that he loved her. He had asked her to marry him, therefore he must love her. It followed naturally.

Her smile had grown radiant and her eyes had glowed as she had looked on a vision of the future. If Nick wanted it this way, with the important things understood but unspoken, then that was the way it would be. She would learn to be as seemingly casual as he, and it wouldn't matter if he never said he loved her because she knew that he did. She must just be careful never to lose sight of that knowledge.

(She had been that much of a stupid, conceited fool, Belle could reflect with a sigh five and a half years later.)

'All right, let's,' she had answered Nick equably and his brilliant smile had flashed out as he had touched her hand lightly.

'Well, welcome back to comedy. God, I can't wait to hear the reaction! That feature you wrote is going to be out of date, isn't it?'

He had ordered champagne, telling the waiter why. Some friends of his were at another table, two distinguished actresses, a playwright and a television producer, and he had insisted on calling them over.

'This is Belle Tyler, soon to be Belle Rosney,' he had introduced her, his eyes alight with wicked enjoyment. 'We've just this minute become engaged.'

Their various stunned reactions had not been exactly flattering to her, Belle had realised, but she was too happy to mind, and Nick was enjoying himself. That was all that mattered. He was a public man, a performer in a sense, so even this first hour of their engagement must be shared with others. The wine waiter had told the proprietor who came forward to proffer his felicitations and eventually everyone in the little restaurant seemed to be celebrating Nick Rosney's engagement.

'If you had any need to advertise, Luigi, you could claim this was the place where Rosney put his neck in the noose,' Nick had joked, devils of amusement glinting in his eyes.

'Oh, hardly, Nick darling,' one of the actresses had protested, her disparaging glance assessing and dismissing Belle, who had remembered that the older woman was rumoured to have had an affair with Nick. 'Luigi doesn't want an entirely female clientele, and that sort of publicity could scare the men off. They might think the disease was catching.'

'And some might hope that it was, darling,' he had countered flippantly, flinging an arm across Belle's shoulders. 'Although I'll grant you it would depend on the lady in question, and there aren't too many Belles around.'

All her life, Belle had thought of herself as an average sort of person, neither plain nor pretty, normally intelligent but nothing exceptional, but Nick made her feel special, beautiful and rare and wonderful. Even if he couldn't tell her directly that she was those things, she felt he believed that she was.

When eventually they had left the restaurant, she had thought that now perhaps he might take her back to his house, but once again he drove her to the shared flat in the sports car he owned and abused. This time, however, when he had kissed her, having seen her into the tiny cramped lounge, he had held her properly, his arms hard and strong across her back, tightening as she had lifted her face to his.

'Nick . . .'

She had shuddered uncontrollably as his mouth moved on hers, wondering why she should have been chosen for so much happiness, and vowing that she would make him as happy as he had her, a silent promise because he would not welcome the utterance of something so emotional, her dear, beloved Nick.

His lips were nudging hers apart and as his tongue stroked delicately over the hot moistness of her inner lip and then probed further, she had felt his hands begin to move over her body, lightly, sensitively, touching the backs of her thighs, her buttocks, waist and back, and then moving down again to caress and hold her hips.

She had stirred sinuously against him, the honeyed languor of desire gradually becoming a sweet pulsing ache that was fiercest deep inside her womanhood but spread sensation through all her being, adding urgency to her restless movements, and she had realised that those strange husky moaning sounds she was hearing came from the back of her own throat, wordless, involuntary little pleas for fulfilment, that she hadn't realised she was capable of making because they were almost animal, arising out of some deep, unexplored and primaeval part of herself that had needed Nick Rosney quite as much as the conscious, thinking, loving Belle Tyler needed him. It was her blood, calling to his in a pounding primitive rhythm and surely, surely, she could not be wrong. He must love her, because how could she love and desire someone so much and not compel, with the very strength of her need, an answering love and want?

Nick had been shaking slightly, his breathing rapid and shallow as he drew back.

'Soon, Belle, very soon?'

'What?'

'Our marriage,' he had reminded her lightly.

'Oh, Nick, I can hardly believe ...' She had stopped, realising she was becoming emotional.

'I did mean it, you know.' He had given her a crooked smile that made her melt.

'Yes.' The word had emerged as a rapturous sigh.

'I think, if you've no objections, that we'd better have a church wedding,' he had continued in his inconsequential way. 'You see, I've an unconscionable number of friends and acquaintances, many of whom would be mortally offended if I failed to invite them to witness our nuptials. After all, it's the joke of the year, and a church is the only way we'll fit them all in.'

It had seemed a strange reason for wanting a church wedding but she had known worse motives less honestly expressed and anyway she would have granted him anything he asked, so she had only touched his darkly handsome face with gentle, loving fingers and acquiesced.

The news had been out in the morning, thanks to the party in the restaurant. When she got to the office, Belle had faced a barrage of questions, and members of the press had either phoned or come to see her throughout the day.

She had coped well. For one thing, they were in a sense her colleagues, asking the questions she would have put in their position, and she knew the answers they wanted to hear. Additionally, believing that she had won Nick Rosney's love gave her a new confidence.

She had kept it light, jokey, knowing that was what Nick, with his aversion to any expression of emotion, would prefer, and the press liked it and played it her way. The only note of sentiment or whimsy was confined to that which had charmed them most, the fact that she had met Nick when she went to interview him, because every one of them had at some stage fantasised about going to interview his or her ideal and staying to wallow in a happy-ever-after ending.

Only one vitriolic lady columnist had remained unenchanted, stating that if it wasn't a publicity stunt, then she offered her deepest condolences to Belle Tyler.

'Sheer disappointment,' Nick had claimed airily when Belle mentioned it to him. 'She also came to interview me once and I omitted to ask her to dinner, let alone marry her.'

'You really are a conceited man,' she had teased, but gently, because those were the days when she had believed him to be a sensitive man, masking real, deep feelings with flippancy.

'I know,' he had agreed unrepentantly. 'You shouldn't have agreed to marry me. It will only make me worse.'

They had been on their way to buy rings and outside the exclusive, famous jewellers, Belle had hesitated.

'Do you also want a wedding ring, Nick?'

He had looked down at her thoughtfully, silent for a while. 'Yes,' he had said eventually, almost mocking himself, she thought. 'Yes, I think I do.'

Her smile had been embarrassed. 'I don't know how these things are done, but . . . Nick, I can't afford one, if I'm supposed to buy it for you. Not at this sort of establishment.'

His eyes had suddenly been alight with laughter as he had hugged her briefly to him. 'You funny girl! Do you think I don't know? I was also a junior staffer, once upon a time.'

Inside the shop, with its tasteful grey décor and laid back proprietor and assistants, one of his outrageous, generous moods had fallen on him. He had wanted to buy her everything she glanced at. Within minutes she had been helpless with laughter while the faintly scandalised jeweller, who had obviously read of their impending marriage and insisted on attending them personally, had patently been torn between good taste and the desire to make a killing.

The engagement ring they had glanced at simultaneously and recognised as perfect, a large square-cut emerald, and the complementary wedding rings were an easy matter, but beyond these, Belle had refused to go.

'Perhaps the matching earrings,' she had allowed eventually because she had pierced ears. 'But no more, Nick. No, I'm serious. I'm . . . too young for this sort of thing. I'm used to plastic and paste.'

He had looked at her and laughed, turning to the jeweller. 'Let her have her way. In a few years' time she'll probably be demanding the Culinan diamond and similar rocks as compensation for putting up with me!'

The jeweller had been almost relieved. 'Emeralds

are definitely her stone, Mr Rosney, but may I suggest diamonds or pearls at twenty-one, and a nice white opal sometime soon if you're not superstitious? Anyone can wear an opal because they're adaptable, taking on the personality of the wearer.'

Nick had been unusually quiet as they left the shop.

'Does the age gap worry you, Belle?' he had asked eventually.

'No, silly!' She had smiled reassuringly, still believing in his sensitivity and thinking that perhaps he was self-conscious about the difference in their ages. 'What's ten years?'

He had laughed abruptly. 'You're a lot more confident than I am, my darling.'

'We'll make it work,' she had promised, buoyant with love and hope. 'You'll see!'

And there, on the pavement, he had hugged her very tightly.

He had taken her to see both sets of parents. Belle's father was the editor of a local newspaper in the Midlands town in which she had grown up. He had admired Nick Rosney and was proud, if startled, that his only child should be marrying him, although he had admitted he hadn't expected her to marry at quite such an early age and urged her not to give up work. Her mother had been much more wary.

'What are you doing with such a man, Belle?' she had asked when Belle was helping her stack the dishwasher. 'That's a man who . . . who has looked at hell, while you—you're eighteen years old and full of ideals. He's——'

'Out of my league?' Belle had suggested good-naturedly, her confidence absolute. 'We love each other, Mum.'

'Well, I just wish you weren't rushing into it this way. Can't you settle for a longer engagement?' Her mother's glance had sharpened. 'Or have you need of haste?'

'No. We haven't ... Nick hasn't——' Belle had hesitated, and gave her mother a shy smile. 'But I think perhaps that's why we need to hurry.'

'Then I suppose he must love you, if he's willing to wait.' Even more idealistic than she believed her daughter to be, she had been smiling. 'So it will be a traditional white wedding? I'm glad, Belle. It's what I've always wanted for you and, in fact, your father and I have regularly been putting something into a savings account we opened for you immediately after your birth, specifically aimed at providing you with either a higher education or a wedding to remember. I know your Nick is very generously expecting to finance the entire affair, but he must at least allow us to give you your wedding dress and a trousseau. There's not much time, though, is there?'

Nick's parents had been a different matter. They lived in Bristol where his father was an English lecturer at the university. His mother was a cool, well-bred woman who kept her house as immaculate as she did her face, hair, nails and clothes. Not a speck of dust lurked anywhere and not a fingerprint marred the many flawlessly gleaming surfaces. Belle, who had opened the car door and stepped out into mud, since it had been raining, was mortified to notice that even though she had wiped her feet carefully, her boots had left a dirty mark on the dove-grey carpet.

'Not to worry.' Nick had grinned, seeing her embarrassment, and reassured her in an undertone which she had suspected he actually meant his mother to hear. 'It will give her something to do when we've gone. She's an obsessive. She cleans the windows every second day and won't trust a char to do any of the work.'

Belle had found them chilly people, perhaps because they were both so self-absorbed, and she had gathered that Nick felt little affection for them. He had told her earlier, in answer to her question, that he visited them occasionally, but she had been faintly shocked to realise during the course of that visit that it had been a full three years since he had last done so.

Certainly, he had little in common with his parents and she had wondered how his temperament had fitted into such a restrained household. Or perhaps his background had shaped that temperament, his occasional outrageousness a reaction against it.

His parents could even be responsible for his inability to express his feelings. Coolly formal and wholly undemonstrative, they would probably deplore any show of emotion.

Their congratulations had been conventional and they had remained aloof, although Nick seemed to have a talent for making them both twitch with irritation, but they remained as outwardly correct and polite as if he were a stranger they were entertaining, as perhaps he was.

The only personal comment had come from his mother as they had been leaving and it had been addressed to Belle. 'You're terribly young, I must say. I hope you know what you're doing. My son can't be easy to live with. He certainly wasn't as a child, as I have cause to remember. He was hyperactive and his moods mercurial. I was at my wits' end, trying to cope. Discipline can only achieve so much.'

'Poor Mother, you must both have wondered how you came by me.' Nick's laughter had been gently malicious as both parents twitched irritably. 'But don't worry about Belle. She's full of confidence!'

'And you, Nick?' Belle had asked softly as they drove away. 'Are you also confident?'

'Me?' He had glanced at her thoughtfully, before smiling. 'I just hope, Belle, I hope.'

It was inevitable that he should be less idealistic than she. The difference in their ages alone would ensure that.

They had seldom been alone together again until after their wedding. Nick had still taken her out every night but now there had been people to meet, famous names and faces who gave parties for them and had looked at Belle with wonder, perplexity and sometimes pity. All Nick's friends had seemed to be well-known personalities but in whatever galaxy she found herself night after night, it had still seemed to Belle that Nick was the scintillating sun around whom they all moved in orbit, such was the charm and power of his personality, and she had known she was falling more and more deeply in love with him.

She had also met people Nick had worked with at one time or another, including the cameraman Graham Thurlow who was to be best man at their wedding, Belle having chosen her pretty ten-year-old cousin for her attendant. She had also met Nick's secretary, Carey Devane, a smooth-haired blonde in her mid-twenties with amethyst eyes and high pointed breasts, who asked Belle how she liked being part of the Nick Rosney Spectacular.

Belle had looked at her, recognising dislike when she saw it, and unsure how to cope with open hostility.

'This latest stunt of his,' Carey had elaborated as she remained silent. 'Getting married.'

'Oh, I see!' Belle had smiled slowly, her eyes going to Nick, gesturing expansively at the other side of the room as he told some story to a titled film director. 'Well, obviously I'm just grateful to have been chosen for a starring rôle, Miss Devane.'

'No, Belle, Nick is the star.' The pretty voice had

been soft and venomous. 'You're the one who ends up with custard in your face.'

She had walked away and Belle had watched the seductive sway of her hips and had felt rather wounded, because she would have liked Nick's friends and colleagues to approve of her. She wasn't stupid, though. She knew jealousy lay behind Carey's antagonism, and she could hardly blame her. She wouldn't mention it to Nick, she had decided. She was the lucky one after all; it was she whom Nick was marrying.

Just for a moment, though, seeing Carey's smooth golden beauty and glancing at all the other sophisticated, accomplished woman in the room, in their gorgeous dresses that had probably cost as much as she earned in a month, she had wondered how she could possibly be the one Nick loved.

'You're looking a trifle distrait, my darling.'

He and Graham Thurlow had come across while she was watching Carey and, looking up into the sparkling blue eyes, Belle had felt all her doubts dispersing. He had asked her to marry him, hadn't he?

'Perhaps she's tired of all this partying and wants to have you to herself for a while,' the bearded cameraman had suggested, his grey eyes kind as they rested on Belle's face. He was one of those who had looked at her with compassion.

Nick's lips quirked. 'Do you?' he had asked Belle.

Belle's slow smile had contained a wry indulgence. 'Well, you are the most sociable person I've ever known. You like a crowd around you, don't you?'

His arm had dropped to her shoulders as he laughed. 'How can we disappoint all these people who are dying to congratulate me and commiserate with you? Keep on smiling, Belle. This time next week, we'll be all alone, on our honeymoon.'

'And where is the honeymoon to be, or mustn't I ask?' Graham had put in.

'Anywhere except in Beirut, I hope, Graham,' Nick had responded promptly. 'Since I'd rather spend my honeymoon with Belle than with you!'

Later, when he had returned her to her flat, Nick had said, 'We haven't actually discussed the honeymoon, have we? I'm not that enamoured of the idea of going away, if you don't mind? I spend so much time travelling in the course of my work that I'd rather take you straight home after the reception. I've told my domestic staff not to come in, so we'll be absolutely alone.'

He had employed an all-purpose manservant as well as a woman who came in to clean four times a week.

'I'd like that,' she had told him amicably.

'We'll go away somewhere if I'm free in the summer,' he had promised.

A little later, his good night kiss had a thoughtful quality, and he had looked at her assessingly as he drew back.

'You are looking strained,' he had commented, apparently unaware that the strain lay in suppressing her desire to cling to him and beg for more than just kisses. He had laughed a little. 'Engagements are notorious as periods of tension. I think that's why honeymoons were invented, to enable people to recover from their engagements!'

She had gone to sleep that night with the consoling thought that within a week she would be his wife, free to show him how much she loved him, even if she couldn't tell him.

She hadn't known how Nick had managed it at such short notice and when neither of them was a member of the particular parish, but somehow he had arranged for them to be married at quite a famous church the following week.

Her mother had come down several times since her engagement, to accompany her on shopping expeditions. Now both her parents, her uncle, her aunt and her young cousin had checked into a modest hotel.

The wedding rehearsal saw Belle giggling helplessly because Nick, aided and abetted by Graham Thurlow, had refused to take it seriously, and eventually even the priest was spluttering with laughter.

She had spent her last evening as a single girl in her parents' suite, barely able to contain her excitement. This time tomorrow, she would be Nick Rosney's wife.

At noon the following day, chaos had reigned in the shared flat. Her mother, flatmates and small bridesmaid had been all fluttery with excitement. Belle and her father had been comparatively calm.

Just for a moment, as she stood beside Nick a short while later, she had wondered what she was doing. He was Nick Rosney, renowned and charismatic, and filling the pews at her back were dozens of women who she had seen looking at him with hungry, covetous eyes, flawlessly beautiful, exquisitely dressed women who, even today, on her day, outshone her in every way. Not even her heavy white velvet gown with its clean flowing lines could make Belle feel that she was anything special.

Then Nick had smiled at her, crookedly, amusement glimmering in the deep blue eyes, and she had shrugged mentally. This was no time to ask for reassurance.

But when it had come to the exchanging of rings, it was Nick's hands that had had a slight tremor, and now Belle's mouth had quirked tenderly as she had wondered wryly if it stemmed from suppressed

emotion or the alcoholic all-male revels of the night
before.

Then as they had been pronounced husband and
wife, she drew a deep breath, elated. Incredibly, she
was now Mrs Rosney!

'We've been and gone and done it now, Belle,' Nick
had mocked in an undertone as he had bent his head to
kiss her, his eyes alight with laughter.

Ah, God, she had prayed with a great surge of love
as his lips touched hers, don't ever let him regret it.

It had never occurred to her that she might be the
one with regrets.

CHAPTER THREE

'WHAT?'

Belle looked up, almost startled to find herself in her tiny office in Taipei with Nick prowling restlessly round her desk. She had been deep in the past, and she hoped she had got through the report to the Canadian network without errors, because for once she hadn't really been concentrating.

Five years on, Nick Rosney's smile was as mocking as it had been on their wedding day.

'*Tempora mutantur*,' he murmured ruefully, pausing opposite her. 'You used to hang on every word I said, didn't you?'

'Did you find it flattering?' Her own smile was self-conscious, but she was usually honest. 'Actually, I was remembering our wedding day.'

'Ah, God, yes!' Nick laughed reminiscently. 'Crazy of us, wasn't it? Do you remember how drunk poor Carey got at the reception?'

'Carey Devane? Yes. What became of her? I don't suppose she's still with you, is she?'

'But she is!'

'I'd have thought she'd married years ago!'

''Can't bring herself to leave me,' Nick claimed flippantly.

She was disturbed. Carey had been one of those women who had looked at Nick with hungry, covetous eyes, and she and Belle had never learned to like each other, but never for a moment during their marriage had Belle doubted Nick's faithfulness. Purely practical considerations had quenched any suspicion of infidelity. When Nick came home, he came to her. Barely in the mood to be a husband, he had certainly been in no mood for an extra-marital affair.

Now, however, she was able to wonder what might have developed in the intervening years.

'How is she?' she questioned him politely.

'You'll be meeting her tonight. As you know, she doesn't usually accompany me when I'm engaged in the practical aspect of my work, but as I've said, this is in the nature of a holiday and I thought she'd enjoy it—particularly this part, the Pacific's own Emerald Isle.'

'I look forward to seeing her again,' Belle claimed courteously and changed the subject. 'What were you saying just now?'

'Nothing important. I was merely commenting on the fact that you've moved around a great deal.'

'Yes.' Belle cursed the too thin skin that made her flush so easily.

Always, wherever she went, she was subject to a sense of dissatisfaction, a feeling that there ought to be something more. After their divorce, she had moved to Bonn where she had perfected her German while working as assistant to an irascible American stringer. After a year, she had saved enough and felt sufficiently competent to branch out on her own. At the end of a five-week holiday at home, she had flown to Sydney from which, making frequent trips to the press gallery in Canberra, she had begun to assemble a respectable list of clients. After another year, however, she had been restless and, inspired by certain films and books, she had moved up to Jakarta to immerse herself in the intriguing political climate there. Terry Whelan, whom she had first known in Sydney, had contacted her from Taipei. His descriptions of the living there had been sufficiently tempting to make her move on as soon as she could afford to do so.

She had arrived at the same time as Travis Schallau, and as Terry and Marilyn McMillan had been looking for two extra people to flat with, they had swiftly become a foursome, living together, united by their careers, tolerating each other's temperaments and, as Travis often said, divided by a common language.

These days, Belle was thinking of moving on to Singapore or Hong Kong.

Her clients complained mildly of her abrupt changes of location but they knew it was the way of reporters and, while she was no genius operating on instinct, she had a certain intelligence inherited from her editor father and the copy she filed was sufficiently newsworthy to prompt them to go on publishing or broadcasting her pieces, mainly political but occasionally done from the human interest angle. Bonuses came when she was commissioned to do something specific, usually a generalised geographical, political or economic feature.

'You make a living?' Nick questioned and then his lips curved sardonically. 'Obviously, since you've never touched the allowance I made you.'

'I've built up a substantial list of clients,' she admitted gently.

'Who?'

'Mostly papers at home, and there's one in Sydney too, plus a couple of bureaux.' Briefly the shadows fled her dark green eyes as she became one professional talking to another. 'But radio has become my favourite medium, Nick. There are actuality-type programmes in just about every English-speaking country in the world that broadcast my reports, and I also do a weekly five-minute report for a German network.'

'I know.' Nick's glance was strangely dark, but then he laughed. 'Radio! Television's poor relation.'

Belle laughed with him. 'Video killed the radio star? Never, Nick!'

'It's strange, though. You should have been the television personality. You're better looking than me.'

The shadows returned. He had always had a facility for such flattering comments but these days she knew better than to think he meant them.

She said abruptly, 'I've finished for the night. Shall we go?'

She glanced at Sue-Ching's desk as she put her finger to the light switch, not for the first time giving thanks for her assistant who, in addition to acting as interpreter for her, made up the accounts and banked the payments which came in a variety of currencies. Next to the telephone department, the foreign exchange desk at the bank was the most important institution in their lives.

'What made you do it?' Nick asked as the elevator carried them down to street level.

'What?' There was a tight breathlessness to her lungs and her stomach fluttered nervously in reaction to his closeness in that confined space.

'This type of reporting,' he elucidated. 'When I knew you, you were all set to work your way up through the hierarchy of your woman's magazine.'

Belle attempted a nonchalant shrug, feeling self-conscious.

'You're not the only one who acts on impulse, Nick. I can't really remember my reasoning at the time, except that I felt I needed a change.'

How could she tell him that she had hoped in this way to understand him, even if it was too late. She had wanted to understand Nick Rosney, the public figure, because the private Nick Rosney did not exist, save as a hollow man. The work wasn't the same as he did, but there were areas of resemblance, notably in the inevitable periods of working under pressure, because when events did explode into something newsworthy, they were usually multi-faceted and there would generally be several aspects to cover simultaneously.

To an extent, it had worked. She felt she knew more of Nick now than she had done during their marriage, and certainly she had developed sufficient imagination to comprehend just how badly she had failed him in her immaturity, even if he had failed her equally with his inability to give her his love.

'And you've no regrets?' Nick questioned her as they stepped out of the lift.

'None. This is what I want to be doing, what I should have set out to do from the beginning.'

'You could hardly be expected to know your own mind at eighteen,' Nick said lightly.

'That's for sure!'

Belle spoke sharply, angered by his assumption that she hadn't known her own mind. She had known both her mind and her heart where he was concerned, and neither had changed. He was the one who had changed his mind, although only in a sense, as he had never made any real commitment to her, either intellectual or emotional. He had married her and made love to her, but those things in themselves didn't constitute commitment. They were mere actions, and she just wished she had realised it at the time.

Darkness had fallen, making the heat bearable, although there was still no hint of coolness in the close, moist air.

'What are you doing about a meal?' Nick asked. 'Knowing my team, there'll be drinks and very little else on offer in my suite, but we could eat somewhere first if you're hungry'

'No, thanks. I usually walk home through the street market along there and buy something to eat from the stalls. It only operates at night,' she added.

She didn't want to share a meal with Nick, just the two of them alone together. It would be too like those other times and she would start remembering again.

Anyway, she had long ago abandoned the practice of three meals a day taken at regular times. She ate if she was hungry and had the time to do so, like so many reporters, sustaining herself with coffee through the long hours of fasting.

'Don't let me prevent you, though,' she added politely. 'I can make my own way to the hotel.'

'I'll come with you,' Nick decided expressionlessly. 'I've heard about these night markets and I'd like to see one.'

'You could film one if you're looking for scenes of the local way of life as illustrative background for your project,' she suggested thoughtfully, interested in his task against her will. 'And one of the ceremonies at which young men drink snake's blood.'

'Ah yes, it's supposed to benefit their virility,' Nick laughed.

'It's an adopted custom, though,' she cautioned. 'They'll tell you that the Japanese are responsible for Taiwan's snake population. You'll find that their ethnic jokes tend to be about the Japanese although they're welcomed in reality because the majority of businessmen and tourists today are Japanese, bringing in foreign currency. But I suppose it's understandable as they were occupied by Japan for fifty years, from 1895 ... Apparently the Japanese were researching serums somewhere in the mountains here and when in 1945 Taiwan reverted to the Chinese, they released all the snakes into the forests.'

At least she and Nick had always been able to

converse with each other in this way, Belle reflected wryly. Just as long as the topic remained impersonal. They both liked people, although she had never needed quite the crowds he required. However, cynical Nick's attendance on war had made him, he still retained the basic extrovert's interest in others, and they were alike in being especially fascinated by the ethos and politics of all peoples, which was probably why they had chosen their particular careers.

They strolled slowly through the market, still talking, and the only disturbing element just then was when she occasionally felt Nick's hand at her back. His touch was so light, barely perceptible, and yet to Belle it was utterly debilitating because it brought back so many memories and while she might be able to thrust them forcibly from her mind, her flesh and blood were traitors, crying out to know again the pleasures of the past.

Taipei was a lively city at night, especially in this sort of area, and the populace thronged the streets. They had to walk mainly in the road, at the mercy of the myriad little motorbikes that were such a prominent feature of Taiwan's traffic, many carrying an illegal load of passengers, as the pavements were occupied by the multitude of stalls. Once Belle had found it bewildering, almost unnerving, to find herself surrounded by a sea of Chinese faces, knowing that few if any of them spoke her language, but now she was accustomed to it. The faces no longer looked all alike and she could speculate about the stories behind the faces and differentiate between Chinese and Taiwanese.

'You've noticed some of the very old ones with that slow walk, the feet barely lifted?' she questioned Nick who was observing everything with interest.

'Yes. Opium?'

'Yes. It's sad, and yet, you know, pure opium smoked through a pipe isn't as evil as the heroin that's made from it. Most of them have lived long lives and gone about their normal business and pleasures every day.'

'Some people might even consider opium beneficial,' Nick commented sardonically. 'Isn't Coleridge supposed to have conceived of Kubla Khan under its influence? I tried it myself once, in Laos, but since no good came of it, nor any bad either, I didn't pursue it.'

Belle felt slightly appalled. Nick always took such risks.

'Is it just recklessness, Nick?' she asked softly. 'Or are you challenging fate for some special reason?'

He looked at her with some surprise. 'After all these years, you're willing to listen?' he taunted gently.

'After all these years, it's no longer quite such an emotional issue, is it?' she retorted coolly because his words had fanned an ember of guilt she had been keeping carefully doused. 'Who wants to be widowed at eighteen? Now I'm no longer a wife, so I can't be widowed, and I can take an academic interest in the matter.'

'Neatly put, Belle.' There was a hard note to his laughter. 'But I miss the little girl whose sole aim in life was to bolster my ego.'

'You killed her, Nick. I buried her.'

'No, she died a natural death,' he disagreed. 'Infatuation is never destined for a long life, is it?'

The long look she gave him was considering, but oddly vulnerable at the same time. There was so much she could have said to correct him. She might even have succeeded in making him feel guilty, although she doubted it. Unable to love, Nick believed that when others claimed to love they were, at best, exaggerating, but more probably lying, either to themselves or to others.

She couldn't tell him. Even if she could convince him ... Well, however flawed he was, Nick was too capable of pity. That great, endless compassion he felt for the starving, the homeless, the broken and bereft, all tragic victims of war and disaster, was the last thing she wanted for herself.

So she only said mildly, 'You haven't answered my question, Nick. But perhaps you don't know the answer yourself?'

'Who can ever know anything like that beyond all doubt?' he retorted with a faint laugh. 'But yes, I think I did go through a stage, a sort of hubris, when I felt compelled to challenge fate and find out just how far I was favoured. Every frontliner experiences that phase if he lasts long enough to start thinking his life is charmed ... You begin to wonder why you're being spared when all around you your colleagues and rivals are being blown to bits. It can be bloody dangerous, thinking you're immortal and that you'll come through it all unscathed. I've been fortunate but not, I now know, specially blessed. I even survived that fate-tempting period and am still untouched today.'

'Well, scarcely untouched,' Belle pointed out, her eyes suddenly haunted. 'You've had a price on your head in Iran, been both shot at and buried under rubble in Beirut, imprisoned in South America and walked without food or water through half Afghanistan.'

All but the first had happened subsequent to their divorce but even so, she had died her own multiple deaths while waiting to hear of his. A world without Nick Rosney in it had seemed a world hardly worth living in, so impoverished would it have seemed.

'But I'm alive, Belle, with my limbs and all my

faculties intact, and that's all that counts,' he laughed. 'I happen to rather . . . like . . . life.'

Momentarily, she was bowed down by the knowledge that he would never change. All his life he would take risks.

Nick saw her hopeless, resigned expression. 'It must have been rough on a romantic, idealistic eighteen-year-old. I had no right to . . . do it to you, no right to—involve you.'

On an impulse, she asked, 'And suppose your luck ran out next week, next month, next year? Nick, if you lost a leg, or your sight? What would your thoughts be then? Would it have been worth it?'

'God, what sort of question is that? When did you become so merciless?' He smiled and grew thoughtful. 'I'd be frustrated, obviously, but I'd find something else to do, and I'd think . . . Yes!'

'Yes, it was worth it. You did what you had to do,' she guessed quietly.

Nick laughed a little. 'The death of your infatuation may have made you unkind to my morale . . . but a whole lot wiser, Belle.'

'I'm just older, Nick.'

'And more experienced.'

'Hardly in the way that you are, though.' She was embarrassed, an acolyte before the priest. 'A bit of bloodletting at riots, but mostly only tear-gas, and being on the wrong side of a couple of governments. Say, rather, more imaginative.'

'Don't underrate yourself,' Nick warned, gently. 'What you're providing is as important as my service, if less well paid.'

It was typical of his generosity but, nevertheless, she wondered silently at the change that had come about. Five years ago, her humility had been such that she could never have spoken to him as she had this evening. It should have been gratifying, but somehow she had felt more at ease in the days when she worshipped at the shrine.

'You . . . honour me professionally, Nick,' she stated rather formally, not knowing what else to say. 'But then, even your request for information for your project did that.'

'And you can help me?'

'I hope so. With notes, certainly.'

'Yes, thank you, but your impressions, Belle? Give me a base to work from, let me know what to look for.' His manner had grown completely professional. 'I know Communist China far better than I do Nationalist China. For a start, for instance, tell me what you most admire about these people.'

'Their industry, their determination to prosper, isolated and in the face of much opposition, their pragmatic exploitation of links with the other . . . pariah states, as you have called them.' Belle paused meditatively. 'But this pragmatism isn't an unrelieved thing, thank God. There's room for great sentimentality and they take an emotional pride in what they are. Have you been to the Chiang Kai-shek Memorial? It's a stunning edifice in its own right and the discipline of the guards is incredible, but it's also a monument to an almost Quixotic idealism. When the idea was first raised, the national budget couldn't run to it, so the people dipped into their own pockets and within a miraculously short space of time the fund was sufficient.'

'I wonder how often they think of all the practical use to which that fund could have been put,' Nick mused sardonically. 'Housing, social services, swelling the defence fund which is obviously a vital matter in a country as vulnerable as this . . . But I don't suppose they'd have contributed quite as generously had donations been requested for any of those things.'

'They think the great man merited such a magnificent tribute. They still love him. Priorities didn't come into it.'

'And I suppose a nation incapable of the occasional prodigality or frivolity would be a pretty boring lot,' Nick added wryly.

Belle glanced at him, thinking he was rather that way himself. Professionally, he had his priorities in good order, his prime commitment being to do his job which, baldly, was to provide the public with facts. Only subordinate to that were all the other things like his eloquent yet never emotive ability to make viewers feel the same anger or compassion that he did.

Away from the events that gave him his living, however, he was capable of extremes of improvidence. She should know, she reflected bitterly. He had even been rashly frivolous enough to marry her, simply to alleviate his temporary boredom!

She stopped at one of the fruit stalls. The fruit in Taiwan was like none she had ever known, luscious nectarines, bright juicy pawpaws, sweet pineapples, and the climate allowed the growth of most kinds. She chose two plums, each big enough to fill her hand, knowing their flavour would match their size, and made the transaction in silence, since the little man selling the fruit knew no English, both of them engaging in holding up notes and folding them in half as they haggled over the price, bargaining being the norm.

She offered one of the plums to Nick, but he shook his head, smiling, and they went on their way, talking idly, and yet still Belle couldn't feel completely at ease with him. Nick was, after all, her ex-husband, he knew her intimately, knew most of her secrets, while she—

she had never really known him, as he had claimed so sardonically when she had found him at the apartment earlier. But she had learnt to know him in the intervening years, through maturity and thought and the remembrance that had kept her company through so many long and lonely nights, and much of what she had learnt was knowledge that disturbed her, awaking both guilt and regret even while she was never free of the awareness that he had never loved her.

She halted in the middle of expounding on the local economy, distracted by the squeal of tyres and a child screaming as two small motorbikes had a coming together. No one was hurt, however, and the two young men were apologising to each other, or perhaps blaming each other, but it sounded too polite for that, while their passengers, obviously their families, stood around, one young mother comforting the little girl who had screamed purely with shock and escaped without injury.

'Christ!'

Belle was more startled by Nick's quiet exclamation than by the collision, such accidents being commonplace, and she looked up at him, a question dying on her lips as she noticed his expression. He was looking exactly as he had that time he had broken her record, eyes ablaze with a dark fire, mouth twisted and the tanned skin of his face stretched tautly over his bones, just as if he were about to give way to an explosive outburst of temper—only this time it wouldn't seem so utterly inexplicable.

So even now she was still learning new things and discovering her mistakes, Belle reflected wryly as she touched Nick's bare arm lightly.

'It's all right. No one is hurt.'

'What?' He turned startled blue eyes on her. Then his face cleared. 'Oh. Yes, of course, The noise . . .'

'Was that why you broke my *1812 Overture?*' she asked, knowing he disliked the personal, but she wasn't as overawed by him as she had been on those days when she had sublimated any inclination that seemed likely to irritate him.

'Oh, God, that! Yes.' His faint laugh was rueful. 'And I used to accuse you of over-reacting.'

Belle's mouth quirked humorously. He had never referred to the incident afterwards, and she had sometimes wondered if he had blanked it out with some form of selective but genuine amnesia.

'You don't like noise, do you?' she persisted, interested to discover if he would try to evade a discussion of his personal hang-ups, especially when a certain sensitivity was implied.

'I hate it,' he answered simply, surprising her. 'In my leisure time, anyway. Especially sudden violent sounds. Some people spout on about the terrible silences of war, and they are terrible . . . You feel so helpless and—exposed, when there should be sound and there isn't. But the noise is far worse. I think. That's why I've never got on with music. It's so violent, especially the classics. Those old composers did it deliberately, I'm sure, to wake audiences up after lulling them to the verge of sleep with a nice soothing passage, the sadistic bastards.'

'And the *1812* comes complete with cannon blasting,' Belle laughed. 'But do you know what's a joke, Nick? The fact that I only brought that record to impress you. I thought my real tastes seemed juvenile to you, and Tchaikovsky was the only so-called classical composer I could appreciate at the time.'

Laughter narrowed Nick's eyes to brilliant slits. 'In retrospect, the whole thing was a comedy, wasn't it?'

A tragi-comedy, she conceded bleakly. But Nick never took anything seriously.

'I suppose so,' she breathed.

Nick ignored the lack of conviction in her tone, asking idly, 'And has your taste in music developed since those days, Belle?'

'Well, I think so,' she said with her slow smile reappearing and gradually becoming laughter. 'But perhaps I'm just compensating for the suppression of my natural tastes back then. Culture Club, Nick.'

He laughed, but then he grew unusually sober. 'I never wanted to force you into trying to become someone you weren't, Belle.'

He had never really wanted her, full stop. Belle's mouth curved ironically, 'You didn't force me, Nick. I was merely stupid enough to try.'

'You didn't try very long, though, did you?' His smile had a diamond quality, blazingly brilliant but sharp and hard as well.

'It was you who mentioned infatuation,' she reminded him tartly.

'Of course. I take it, then, that in your subsequent— adult—relationships, you've felt free to be yourself?'

'Relationships?' Belle repeated carefully. 'Just how many am I supposed to have had, Nick?'

'Well, one or two at least, surely.' He sounded surprised. 'It has been five years, after all.'

'I suppose you've had dozens?' She hated the censure and curiosity she heard in her own voice. How pathetic could she get?

'I haven't exactly bothered to count,' Nick replied easily. 'Have you? Who's your current man, Belle? Schallau?'

'Travis?' Belle was beginning to have an uneasy feeling that the American correspondent was about to become one of those nagging little problems that so often troubled her conscience. Quite a few nice men had been attracted to her in the last five years and she always felt guilty over her inability to return their interest. 'Now why have you hit on him and not on Terry Whelan?'

'Have I got it wrong? Certain things led me to assume that Whelan's interest was in the New Zealand girl, and Schallau's in you. He followed you to your bedroom back at the apartment, didn't he?'

'And that makes an affair? At eighteen I might have made something of having a man in my bedroom,' she taunted. 'But Travis and I aren't exactly adolescents. We've both been married, for heaven's sake.'

'And you both have natural needs, presumably. Is he your lover?'

'No.' She stood still and Nick stopped walking, turning to look at her.

'No? Or no, not yet?' He was infuriatingly confident that she would confide in him.

'Do you have the right to know?'

'No, of course not, but why shouldn't you tell me?' Nick was surprised. 'You can't have anything to be ashamed of . . . I'll tell you about my affairs if you like; those I can remember. Some were rather . . . brief.'

'Actually, Nick, I'm not particularly interested.' Belle would never know how she managed to sound so coolly indifferent when inwardly she was seething, hurt and jealousy and rage and humiliation all combining to create a horrible, sickening inner turbulence. 'Shouldn't we be getting along to your hotel, now that I've had something to eat?'

'That was your meal? Two plums? No wonder you're so thin.'

'You could have said—slim,' she protested resentfully.

'Slender.' Nick gave her a lazy grin. 'Actually, I rather like it, but you have overdone it slightly, you know.'

Belle felt as if her heart stopped when she saw the way he was looking at her and her rejoinder was never uttered. Nick's eyes were moving slowly over the taut slender lines of her figure. Even in her fairly loose dungarees, the smallness of her waist was evident, making her breasts look fuller although, in fact, she took a smaller size in bras than she had five years ago. Belle saw something kindle in the vivid eyes as they moved upward and she experienced a familiar sensation of warm, pleasurable weakness, beginning in the secret regions only he had known but spreading through all her body and limbs.

No, she thought in anguish, and her internal muscles spasmed as if in resistance to the memory of his possession.

'We should be going,' she murmured, a little breathless.

'Yes.'

He smiled, moving closer to her, and bent his dark head to kiss her mouth lightly, so lightly that it was hardly a proper kiss at all, just a warmth and a movement against her lips which trembled in involuntary response.

'Let's go.' He was still smiling.

'What did you do that for?' she demanded huskily as they started walking again.

Nick moved a shoulder. 'I'm not sure. It was just an impulse.'

A bitter anger choked her. 'I'd have thought you'd have learned not to yield to impulse by now, Nick,' she claimed tightly. 'Remembering that impulse once led you to marriage and divorce.'

The look he gave her was full of impatience but his drawling words made her suspect that it was directed at himself.

'A timely reminder, Belle. Thank you.'

Just then, she could almost hate him, because the touch of his lips on hers had unlocked a door, and a welter of memory was swamping her, physically as well as mentally as her body recalled how it had been for them, especially that first time, because in her case, the old cliché was true—the first time had been the best.

CHAPTER FOUR

BELLE had noticed nothing wrong that first time.

She had been too lost in a sea of sensation, drowning in the sweet, frantic excitement induced by Nick's hands and mouth and body as he guided her gently on a journey of discovery that was like scaling a mountain of unimaginable height, only easily, effortlessly. He had been so patient, almost needlessly so, letting her pause to revel in the rapture of it each time she thought that now, surely, they had attained the peak of physical passion, before leading her on to further discoveries, to fresh heights of sensual pleasure, until she felt she must lose her mind, because her wildest imaginings had never conceived of such perfect rarefied altitudes.

Their wedding reception, held at a very famous hotel, had been a scintillating affair, not merely lustrous but a-sparkle with the brilliance of a multitude of glitterati, and through it all, through all the competitiveness, as star strove to outshine star, Nick Rosney, the bridegroom and host, had still blazed the brightest and, utterly besotted, Belle had been content to be a pale shadow at his side.

'I enjoyed that,' he had commented, driving her home after a mildly riotous send-off. 'Did you?'

'It was . . . interesting, but——' She had looked at him, relaxed and humorous, and decided to risk a little emotion. 'I'm glad to be going home with you, Nick.'

'Yes. In small doses, they're all enchanting people, but after a while they can become a bit wearing,' he had conceded, either not recognising the emotion or

61

else skipping out of its path and at the same time issuing her with a subtle warning not to labour it.

The house was immaculate when they had arrived, thanks to his staff, but Nick had soon changed that. Already Belle had known how untidy he was. Somehow debris seemed to accumulate wherever he happened to be, and she thought that was probably what came of having a fanatically houseproud mother.

They had each had another glass of champagne, more because it had been left for them than because they had wanted it, and then Belle had gone upstairs to the master bedroom, to which her cases of clothes and a few other personal possessions had been transported earlier that day. Her books and records had been left downstairs, she had noticed. Her record-player she had bequeathed to her flatmates as Nick had had his own sophisticated stereo equipment which, he had told her, he only used if he gave a party, preferring television and radio. In his car, he had played only *Monty Python* tapes or listened to news bulletins.

The bedroom had been comfortable, discreetly luxurious, all in fairly neutral shades, so that it hadn't dominated, but had allowed one to impose one's own personality. Someone, either Nick or his manservant, had cleared at least two thirds of the cupboard and drawer space for her and, discovering it, Belle had laughed somewhat nervously. Even with her new trousseau, she hadn't owned enough to utilise all that space.

Then her expression had grown serious. It had been dark outside, but still early, and she had wondered how many hours she had still to wait before she and Nick would consummate their marriage.

She had still been wandering about the room,

somewhat helplessly, when Nick had appeared at the door.

'Belle, I never thought!' His expression had been ruefully contrite. 'We've been left a meal for tonight which only needs heating, but otherwise ... I hardly expect you to cook on your honeymoon so we can either eat out or send out, or we can exist on steaks and baked potatoes which are about my limit. There's plenty of drink and tea and coffee in the house, however. Do you know, after all the meals we've had together, I still don't know what you like best!'

'Scrambled egg with a glass of sherry,' she had answered promptly, and stopped. 'Nick?'

Somehow their eyes had caught, and held, and something in Nick's gaze had told Belle that her time of waiting was over. There was a warmth, and an awareness, in his glance as it travelled over her, and she had known that she had been looking her best, probably better now than she had done in her wedding gown, in the softly clinging pale apricot two-piece, belted at the waist, and with her hair down once more.

'Let me undress you, Belle,' he had requested quietly.

'Yes,' she had breathed, taking a step towards him.

'Now?'

'Yes.' She had been smiling. 'Ah, Nick, I thought ... I was wondering when ...'

'I've wanted to,' he had confessed deeply, his hands cupping her face. 'But I had to wait.'

He had filled his hands with the smoothly shining mass of her hair and then let its silken weight spill over her shoulders as he had bent his face to hers, kissing her cheeks and the bridge of her nose before coming to her lips. His kiss had been slow, almost languorous, deepening only gradually into a warm, unhurried exploration of her mouth, and Belle had trembled uncontrollably and had clung to him.

Still with no trace of impatience, he had drawn back to untie her belt, and she had wondered a little at his control when already she was a helpless, quivering mass of love and longing. But of course, he was experienced . . .

His undressing of her had been a leisurely process, with many pauses to look at her, to kiss her and touch her, her face and hair and the flesh he was exposing in stages, with an infinitely tender sensuality.

And all the while he had talked to her, lightly and inconsequentially, mostly about their wedding reception, recalling incidents that had amused him—almost, Belle had reflected with slightly hysterical humour, as if this were an ordeal from which her mind needed distracting, instead of the coming together she had been hungering for.

Her dentist chatted to her in just such a way when she was in the chair!

'Funny things, wedding receptions,' he had murmured against a highly sensitive region of her neck, just below her ear, while his fingers had been busy with the fastening of her bra, and Belle had found it difficult to concentrate on what he was saying. 'They're such alcoholic occasions. Even Carey was drunk today. Did you notice?'

'Yes.' Belle hadn't wanted to talk about Carey Devane. 'Nick, can I . . . can I undress you as well?'

'In a minute,' he had said absently, lifting his head with a quick smile.

He had drawn back to look at her breasts, and then he had begun touching them, fingertips lightly tracing patterns all over the soft, smooth mounds of flesh, moving in apparently random little circles, that had still brought him closer and closer to the rose-dark centres, and Belle realised she was holding her breath.

Then a choking little sound of ungovernable pleasure had escaped her as Nick's fingers, skilled and sure, had closed about her nipples, gently plucking at them, teasing them into stiff erection, and she had made a violent, involuntary movement, flinging back her head while her hands had gone to Nick's midnight hair, drawing his face down to hers.

He had still had himself well under control, but it was the first time a man had ever touched her breasts and Belle was wildly out of control and incapable of hiding it. She shook so violently, tearing at Nick's clothes, and he had had to help her, but when they both stood naked she felt a little shyness return because he had been so very, essentially, male, strong and hard and vital and ... She had swallowed convulsively. He had also been unutterably beautiful, too beautiful for her, and she hadn't known how she had merited this joy, the fulfilment of becoming his wife and, now, his lover.

Nick had looked back at her, his eyes bright and alert.

'Belle, you are ... This is the first time, isn't it?'

'Yes.' She had flushed and his mouth had quirked as he had drawn her to him.

He had held her close against the hard length of him for a short while, doing nothing else, allowing her time to absorb what it was to feel a man's naked body touching hers, but when her hips had begun to move restlessly in involuntary response to the demand implicit in his hardness, he had stirred, looking over her shoulder.

'We have a bed waiting to be used,' he had murmured. 'Come and lie down, darling.'

Soon Belle had been utterly mindless, gasping and

frantic, as the tension had built, becoming intolerable, and pleasure had given way to rapture and a need that was pain, and ache deep inside her where a throbbing space awaited his manhood, crying out to contain him, and only him, because he was the one she loved and would always love, and her femininity had been created for him to fill, and no other.

And still Nick had continued to exercise that exquisite restraint, even after he had found the evidence of her readiness to receive him. The warm sensual slide of his mouth had been an erotic torment, exploring every inch of her feverish body but always returning, again and again, to her tumescent breasts. His hands too had contributed to her frenziedly wanton desire as they had moved on her, fondling her breasts, stimulating them, stroking down over the length of her body and thighs to her knees, and then gliding up the silken length of her inner thighs, to hold her there, where she had wanted him, and moving on, a magician's hands, gently massaging, caressing . . .

Belle had not been able to stifle her husky little whimpers of delight at each new touch, each new way of kissing. He had been doing this to her, for her, she had thought wildly, taking the time to pleasure her in this way first, when his swollen need had evidenced his own readiness to claim her in the ultimate way, and somehow it had been incredible to think that he had cared that much.

'Nick!' she had called to him urgently, wanting to excite and please him in return. 'Nick, let me touch you too . . . like that.'

His eyes had been intent as he had looked down at her passion-racked body and her head that thrashed restlessly from side to side on the pillows, her long hair tangled.

'Yes.' The smile he had given her had been quick and tight.

He had taken her hands in his, drawing them to his body and guiding them over its length from his chest, with its tangle of dark hair, down to the taut flatness of his stomach and the hardness of his thighs, teaching her what he had wanted and then leaving her to revel in her discovery of the pulsating tension at the demanding, commanding core of his being, while her lips too began to make discoveries, the last of her inhibitions having fled.

'Enough now, Belle.' He had stopped her after a short while, drawing her back to him, holding her body very close to his before pushing her gently on to her back and she had known that the time had come. The waiting was over.

'Please, Nick, please!' she had begged urgently, eyes tight shut as he had paused above her, then had slid between her waiting thighs.

He had been shaking and she had said his name again as he had grasped her hips, raising her, and she had felt him move against her.

Her fingers had dug into his shoulders as he had taken her, and what had followed had been a revelation, a miracle. Never until now had Belle fully realised how perfectly the two sexes complemented each other, the differences between them made for each other's delight. She hadn't been able to contain her moans of pleasure as she had felt Nick moving within her and a pulsating internal rapture begin in response to the deep rhythmic strokes of his possession.

Her eyes had flown open, and she had looked up into Nick's dark face, sheened with a fine film of perspiration, his black hair falling over his damp brow. His eyes had been glazed and blind, and his face had seemed all sharp angles, the skin stretched tautly over the bones, with a flush lying along his high cheekbones, while his mouth had been a tightly compressed line.

'Nick!'

She had been almost afraid to yield to the mounting rapture, frightened of letting go because he would take her, spiralling up and up, to a place she had never been before, a realm of sensation where she would lose her mind and die a death of ecstasy.

'Don't fight it, darling,' he had grasped. 'Let it happen.'

She had heard him and obeyed, her sharp cries of joy filling the room as her pleasure had approached a soaring crescendo and Nick had lifted her up to a towering pinnacle of ecstasy, exquisite and undreamt of. As he had filled her with his life force, she had called his name once more in a final rictus of the pure, perfect ecstasy that so closely resembles agony, before floating lightly back to earth, weightless through the darkness to a warm well of deep, tranquil contentment, so utterly sated that it felt as if she had lived all her life and attained such total fulfilment that she could now die complete and happy, and in fact had felt in a way as if she were dying softly and satisfyingly.

A long time later, when her mind had started working once more and she had been alone with her thoughts for a while, Belle stirred.

'Nick?'

He had moved away from her almost immediately and switched out the light, and now he lay on his back at her side, with a space of several inches between them.

'I'm here.'

'She had levered herself up on one elbow and had leaned towards him but hadn't touched him, although she had meant to, some extra, unreasoned sense of him coming into play and preventing her from doing so, because he had created a space about himself which she might not violate.

'Nick,' she had ventured, husky with emotion and wanting to find some way of thanking him. 'It . . . I never guessed, I never knew how . . . how it was . . .'

'I know, darling,' he had confirmed gently. 'But don't talk about it, all right?'

'Yes, but . . .' She had searched for words. 'What about you, Nick? Was it . . . all right for you?'

'It was as perfect as I'd hoped,' he had reassured her with lazy tenderness, putting out a hand to caress her hair but withdrawing it almost at once. 'But no more, now, please, Belle.'

He was right; what they had just shared was something beyond words, she had decided. All the same, for a few fleeting moments, she hadn't helped wishing that he might have held her in his arms and told her with words that he loved her, now, in this quiet time. But obviously he was a man who needed to isolate himself . . . afterwards, after the ultimate closeness.

But she had all of him to which she was entitled, she had reminded herself. His soul wasn't hers to ask for, and if he couldn't express himself in the things that mattered . . . Well, that was Nick Rosney and she loved him as he was, not as he might be.

A little later, she had moved again.

'Did you say something about a meal earlier?' she had questioned him with a smile in her voice. 'Because I'm starving, Nick!'

He had laughed and snapped on the light. 'So am I!' He had got up and gone over to the walk-in cupboard, emerging with a robe. His eyes had gone to her still unpacked suitcases standing just inside the door. 'I suppose you've got something white and frothy that you were supposed to wear?'

Belle's lips had curved with wry tenderness. 'My mother insisted.'

'She's a romantic, isn't she?'

And that was something she herself must learn not to be, Belle had reflected. She hadn't yet doubted Nick's unspoken love for her, but already she had known she must not expect him to dress it up in romance.

Later that night, Nick had made love to her again and, looking back, Belle knew that had been when her first real doubts were born. That first time had been too novel an experience for her to analyse the degree of Nick's participation in any real depth. She had only known that his prime intention had been to pleasure her, and she had accepted his generosity as her due. As a virgin, she had merited such consideration.

Now, however, she had wanted to return to him some of the joy he had given to her; she had wanted to ensure that he received as much as he gave.

It hadn't worked. That second time, and all the other times in the days and nights that had followed, she was to notice that Nick's involvement in the act of love had been nowhere near matching hers, which was total. Always there had been that restraint, or reserve, and he had maintained the habit of talking about unrelated matters during the foreplay that left her breathless and trembling.

She began to notice that he never made a sound during their couplings, and he was never shaken afterwards, as she had been. In fact, after that first time, he had always left the bed and the room afterwards, as if he had needed to extend the space he occupied, and so she lay alone, realising with dawning horror that the uninhibited abandon of her responses had probably disgusted him.

Quite simply, Nick had never, ever, lost control, and her awareness of it made Belle self-conscious, so that she had learnt in swift stages to temper her responses, devising a control of her own.

Within days of their marriage, she had been feeling the strain. It was killing her, trying to maintain the charade of being as coolly unmoved as Nick when they made love, endeavouring to stifle her groans of desire and cries of joy at his possession, and resisting that final scintillating explosion of ectasy at the peak of each union. Only embarrassment at the prospect of Nick's witnessing her complete loss of control while he was still so very much in control had enabled her to keep on dissembling.

But she hadn't known how much longer she could keep it up. The trouble was, Nick's most perfunctory caress was able to arouse her to such a pitch of desire that she became mindless, swamped with passion, but she had no similar effect on him. That was the part which had hurt, and Belle spent a considerable amount of time brooding over that humiliating imbalance.

She would just have to learn to live with it, she had supposed sadly, late one night when Nick had left the room after making love to her. Later he would return, she knew, and sleep beside her, but without touching her, and in the morning they would probably make love again.

She must simply accept that while she loved Nick, he didn't—But no, she wasn't going to let that sort of doubt creep in, she had vowed. He had married her, and at least he bothered to make love to her, even if he didn't quite abandon himself as wholeheartedly as she longed to do. Of course he loved her. He just didn't love her quite as much as she did him. That was the thing she had to learn to accept.

But she went on longing for some sort of affirmation. He was her first lover and she was eighteen and increasingly unsure of herself, where once she had been full of confidence.

It had been no use trying to persuade Nick to talk it over with her, however. He had been adroit at turning the conversation if ever she attempted to initiate such a discussion, indicating gently but inexorably that he wanted to keep their conversations on an impersonally superficial level.

Perhaps he hadn't wanted to have to hurt her with the truth, Belle had reflected occasionally—because it was too late for vows of faith. Doubt had already become her cruel master, flawing almost every moment of the time she had spent with Nick.

But he had married her, she had reminded herself desperately, a hundred times a day, only now it was no longer sufficient reassurance. She had needed more and since he couldn't tell her he loved her and didn't show her with his restrained lovemaking, she sought for other proofs—and found pitifully few.

Nick had been kind and entertaining, but he had made her no speeches about love and, beset by uncertainty, Belle had now been too nervously inhibited to ask a direct question and insist on an answer. Anyway, she hadn't been sure she had wanted to hear that answer.

'Why do you talk so much?' she had asked once, trying to keep her tone teasing, but it was difficult when Nick had filled his sensitive hands with her breasts and was massaging them to taut, swollen fullness, the nipples distended and hard, like fiery peaks of marble—and at the same time he had been recounting a comically macabre incident in which he had once been caught up in in Morocco.

'Do I?' Nick had looked startled. 'I hadn't realised . . . Don't you like it? Would you rather we proceeded in silence?'

As if it were some routine exercise they were engaged in, she had thought unhappily, trying to smile back at him.

'No, of course not. I was just wondering, because you never talk about anything related to . . .' Belle had hesitated and had decided to risk seeing his face tighten with irritation. 'Why do you never talk about . . . about us, Nick?'

'Is that the voice of your ego speaking?' To her surprise, his smile had grown teasing. 'Well, what do you want to hear about yourself, my darling? That you're lovely, and sexy, and . . .'

'Nick . . .' She had stirred restively, but could voice no protest. When he smiled at her like that, with his eyes alight with affectionate laughter, his charm was absolute and she became his happy slave. Never mind that it was only affection she found brightening the blue eyes instead of smouldering love and passion. That was Nick, incapable of being serious, and she loved him.

'And the most beautiful hair I have ever seen,' he had continued lazily, lifting the silken strands in his hand, kissing them and letting the smoothness slip through his fingers. 'Truly your crowning beauty, Belle . . . Belle who is beautiful.'

'It's a nuisance, really,' she had murmured.

'Promise me you'll never cut it?'

Looking up at him, and feeling his body stirring against hers, she had only been able to smile and murmur languidly, 'I promise.'

'Ah . . . Belle!' He had said her name like an exclamation, still smiling.

'Beau!' she had retorted and they had both laughed,

one of the sweet times when her doubts had dissolved because she was here alone with him, his chosen wife, with no one else to intrude, and they were laughing together.

But then laughter had fled as Nick returned his attention to her breasts and she had pressed her lips tightly together to prevent a cry of pleasure as his thumb and fingers curved about one of the smooth mounds, lifting her breast to meet his descending mouth, his warm breath fanning her sensitised flesh. Even so, a low choked moaning sound had come from the back of her throat as his lips had opened over her breast and she had felt his tongue snaking about her engorged nipple, slow and sinuous and infinitely seductive, destroying her control. Ah, God, why did his lovemaking have to be so utterly, accomplishedly, debilitating even when he was maintaining that hurtful reserve, continually holding something back from her?

A little later, as he had spilled himself into her, it was all she had been able to do to prevent herself from shrieking softly as ecstasy had spasmed through her, and her fists had clenched above her head, clutching at the softness of the pillows as fiercely as she had hung on to her self-control.

It was incredible, she had thought anguishedly as they lay side by side but apart once more, their loins still damp from their lovemaking, that Nick could be withholding so much and still be such a potent lover.

Because she had known he was keeping part of himself from her when he possessed her.

Doubt had flooded back. Perhaps he talked in that light manner during the initial phase of their physical encounters because he was bored but felt duty bound to provide her with the caresses, the erotic arousal, before possessing her.

Suddenly, as Nick had got up and gone away, Belle

had known she had to give in and at least consider the darkest possibility, the very worst scenario her lack of confidence could create. Then perhaps she would be able to laugh at the ludicrousness of it and in doing so find reassurance and renew her belief in Nick's love.

The trouble was, when she was done, it all seemed so plausible. Belle didn't have a wild imagination; she confined herself to real possibilities and soon had her answer because now that she reflected on it, it seemed that Nick had scattered clues all along the way.

It was all too likely, now that she knew him a bit better, that he had taken her out and married her for the sheer hell of it. She had been a novelty, something to shock his friends with, a naïve, adoring eighteen-year-old, not even beautiful, the complete antithesis of all the women who normally peopled his private life.

And, inevitably, the mood had passed and he had regretted the whim. He could even have done so before their wedding, but kindness perhaps, or pride because the announcement had been made, with its ensuing publicity, had forced him to go through with it.

Either way, he was now caught in a trap of his own making.

Nick was an intelligent man, she knew, and while he was somewhat cynical, he was not an unkind person. He would never be cruel or inflict deliberate suffering on her, his foolish worshipper, she was sure.

He would have the wit to view her as the essentially innocent victim of his impulse. He could not doubt her love for him and so he probably felt he owed her some semblance of happiness. That was why he was now forcing himself to make contained, dutiful love to a woman he didn't really desire.

She hadn't wanted to believe it—she had refused to!

But Belle wasn't stupid. It had fitted so appallingly

well, explaining so much. His inability to articulate his love she had been able to accept, expecting him to express it in his possession of her but, while he was capable of giving her, over and over again, a rapture of incredible range, undimensioned because it was boundless, she had known that he himself experienced no such ecstasy. His involvement in the act of love, so-called, was only partial, a token performance.

And she hadn't known what to do, what line to take. She had lacked the confidence to believe she could make him come to love her in time, especially as he obviously wasn't sexually dependent on her, but on the other hand, she suspected she had too much pride to settle for long for the hollow, pitying imitation of love which he seemed prepared to offer her.

And for how long? The time must come when he would feel the need to be ruthless and move on, or would he resort to subterfuge in order not to disillusion her too soon?

If only she could get back to that phase when her confidence in his love had been absolute—and if only Nick would give her some sort of proof of his love.

Belle had gone on searching for proofs, subtly trying to prompt them, but none had been forthcoming.

The telephone call had come when their marriage was five days old, as they had both known it must. Nick had been tuning in to news bulletins and making constant telephone calls, monitoring a certain situation, and now a stage was reached when he must go.

Normally she would have accepted unquestioningly the need for him to depart. Her own professional sphere of existence touched the perimeters of his, and she knew what was involved, but the tension and anxiety of the last few days prompted her to choose this occasion to challenge, once more, the extent of his commitment to her.

'Why must you go?' she had asked somewhat petulantly, watching him pack a couple of changes of clothing.

'You know I have to,' he had replied, impatient and rather disconcerted, obviously having expected her to understand.

'But this is our honeymoon,' she had protested. 'Let someone else go. You've got assistants, Nick. Let one of them gain experience and get the kudos.'

'I want to go, Belle,' Nick had retorted, drawling.

'But you'll be in danger, taking risks——'

'Let me explain to you——'

'I don't want to hear,' she had flared angrily, because he hadn't even been looking at her. 'It seems to me that your work means more to you than I do.'

'Don't be childish, Belle.' He had never spoken to her so coldly, and she had been silenced for a while, but when she had followed him out to his car, genuine fear surfaced and she had spoken spontaneously.

'Take care, Nick! Mind how you go, please! And come back to me.'

The smile he had given her had been brilliant, but he had driven away without a word.

He was probably relieved to be getting away from the need for pretence, she had speculated bitterly. He was escaping.

Strangely, she, too, had felt relieved. His absence would give her time to think, and perhaps the breathing space would allow her to find the wisdom and strength to cope when he returned.

CHAPTER FIVE

THEY hadn't really had a chance, Belle knew more than five years later. The pity of it was that she hadn't realised it at the time. Had she done so, she could have spared herself months of anguish.

And Nick would have been spared a great deal of irritation.

The acknowledgement awoke an old pain. It had been one of the most humiliating aspects of their relationship, the fact that within a very short space of time, Nick's prime emotion with regard to her had been a sort of irritated impatience.

It had been inevitable. Belle looked across the room to where her dynamic ex-husband was dazzling two lovely women with his facile charm, an incredibly handsome man flanked by the pulchritude he merited, the conventional golden-haired beauty of Carey Devane and the more unusual attraction of a tall woman of about thirty whose dark hair was skilfully cropped to emphasise the elegantly classical shape of her head, while her grey eyes were so clear and shining that they had the quality of crystal.

Belle sighed unconsciously. Even today, with her adult slenderness and the delicate bone-structure of her face far more evident than it had been five years ago, she knew she hadn't a hope of competing with such women.

She just wondered what it was that had made her go on enduring, throughout the six months of their marriage—the stupid, groundless, optimism of her extreme youth, or some sort of emotional masochism.

'Belle? It really is you?' The cameraman Graham Thurlow stood beside her, still bearded, still kindly.

'Graham! So you're in on this trip,' she exclaimed with quiet pleasure.

'God, it's great to see you again after all this time. But, I confess it, I hardly recognised you when you walked in with Nick. You've changed so much!'

'I should hope so,' she laughed. 'I was a real chubby chops back in the days when we became acquainted, wasn't I?'

'I thought you were rather sweet.'

'Sweet?' Her mouth twisted wryly. 'Graham Thurlow, you don't deserve to hear this, but—I recognised you instantly. You haven't changed a bit!'

'Ah, Belle, the things you do for my ego,' he teased. 'At forty, I'm supposed to be heading for the male menopause, riddled with insecurity and mourning the passing of my youth.' He paused, sobering. 'I was sorry when you and Nick split up, my dear.'

'Sorry, but unsurprised,' Belle guessed knowingly, remembering the sympathy with which he had looked at her in those days.

'Well, I know he can't be the easiest person in the world to live with, with his volatile temperament. Hell, I don't think he finds himself easy to live with, especially when he's at leisure. That's what makes him so restless and unpredictable, I suppose.'

'He hasn't changed, has he?' she queried rather flatly.

'Hardly at all, really,' Graham confirmed thoughtfully.

'Well, there's nothing much there to undergo any changes anyway.' Watching him with those two women, accepting Carey's adulation as if it were his due and giving nothing but his facile, empty charm in return, was increasing Belle's feeling of bitterness and she could not prevent the sardonic words from spilling out.

'I don't get you.' Graham looked at her enquiringly.

'He's a hollow man, Graham, haven't you ever noticed? He has got nothing to give.'

'You're wrong there, you know, Belle,' he disagreed gently. 'In one sense, he has a hell of a lot to give and, in fact, he gives beyond his reserves. You have to remember that he's essentially a fieldman. Even this sort of project doesn't really satisfy him. He was born a fieldman and he'll die one, I'm afraid. That will never change.'

'And the dying will probably occur right there in the field, as you euphemistically call it,' she retorted in a hard voice, because the old fear for Nick had never left her. 'War zones, the frontline.'

'At the risk of sounding corny, it's the way he'd want it, love. I don't think he can imagine any other death. But——' Graham was looking serious and concerned. 'Was this what came between you two, Belle? His job?'

'No, not really.' She gave a self-conscious little laugh, embarrassed at realising how much hurt she must be revealing and wondering why she was talking like this. 'I think I just used it as an excuse, because it was something tangible, something to protest against, whereas the other things weren't. You see, I've always understood Nick's professional commitment and I would have accepted it if . . . If only he had also made some sort of commitment in his personal life, but he gave . . . very little, each time he came home, Graham.'

'And you were a vulnerable eighteen, in need of lots of reassurance,' he reasoned sympathetically. 'But did it ever occur to you that when he came home it was from the war zones, where tension runs high? He probably had nothing left to give for a while and by the time he started feeling human again, it would be time for him to take off once more. The cycle is familiar. Strain is a considerable factor. Someone researched this seriously after the Falklands and it was found that stress was highest among the media men accompanying the task force because they had no common cause to unite them into a cohesive body but were directly in competition with each other.'

Belle sighed. She knew all that. Everyone seemed to make excuses for Nick, because he was a genius, doing a difficult and dangerous job. Her own father had exonerated him with similar phrases.

She would just have to let them think she had been too selfish and immature to cope, as she had been in a way, because she could hardly describe in her own defence Nick's lack of true passion when they made love which, coupled with the absence of any verbal admission of feeling, had added up to the inescapable fact that he simply hadn't been in love with her.

Already she had said too much, and she was angry with herself. It had been in bad taste to reveal as much as she had.

Travis Schallau came over to join them and Belle welcomed him smilingly, relieved at being able to divert Graham by introducing him to the American.

'D'you always work with Rosney?' Travis asked him.

'Generally, but not always. In the sort of situation we cover, it's best to have a tried and tested team. That way we know on which feet the corns are. But this time around, being a project of a somewhat different nature, we've quite a few new faces and, in fact, even if something blows up and calls for Nick's departure, I'm scheduled to complete this series with his assistant.'

'Who is?' Belle asked interestedly, glancing round the hotel room to see who she could identify.

'Deborah Palmer,' Graham supplied.

'One of the women?' Travis grinned. 'All right, I'm impressed. Which?'

'The dark one with brains as obvious as her beauty,' Graham laughed.

'And the fair one is an assistant of another kind, Travis,' Belle informed him darkly. 'She's his secretary, or personal assistant, or whatever.'

'Way to go,' Travis murmured softly, nodding his head and looking at Nick and the two women admiringly. 'Why didn't I go into television? If those are the perks!'

Belle turned to Graham, unable to quench her curiosity although she thought she managed to keep her tone light, 'Tell me, Graham, did Carey ever get what she wanted from Nick?'

'She wanted what you got and tossed away. Marriage, my dear,' Graham retorted, but his smile was compassionate. 'But I do understand what you're asking me. Nick doesn't confide in me, but I think, perhaps, yes, for a very short time, two or three years ago. I'm not sure whether it's pitiable or admirable that she should have gone on working for him afterwards.'

'I don't suppose Nick ever thinks about it,' she returned acidly. 'But Graham, let me get this clear? You're saying that they are not, currently, lovers?'

'Precisely,' he agreed and she despised herself for the surge of relief that coursed through her. 'If he has a roommate on this trip, it has to be Deborah. Not that Carey is exactly thick, but where Nick and women are concerned, all things bright and beautiful has always been his policy.'

Especially after his rash, aberrant marriage to a

complete dodo, Belle thought resentfully, turning away from Graham and Travis, who hardly noticed because they were already talking about something else.

She didn't want Deborah Palmer and Nick to be lovers, and the knowledge that they probably were was making her feel wounded and petulant. She also felt furious with herself for being so stupidly childish. At her age, she ought to be more realistic and able to accept facts. She had no rights where Nick was concerned, no claim on him, and she was being as juvenile in wishing there was no Deborah Palmer as she had been in childhood when she hadn't wanted Christmas to be over or Monday to follow Sunday.

Dear God, hadn't she learnt yet and hadn't Nick's reappearance in her life supplied ample confirmation that she had never meant anything much to him? He couldn't have come back with so little rancour, regarding their marriage as a rather silly joke, had he cared for her in any way at all.

Anyway, he was incapable of caring deeply about anyone. She knew that, didn't she, so where was the use in expending emotion in this futile way? She was supposed to be a rational adult; she ought to be able to accept the inevitable.

Suddenly restless and dissatisfied, she glanced around the crowded lounge of the hotel suite, wanting to escape both her thoughts and this environment. Everyone else seemed cheerfully content, and some hard drinking was underway. No one would notice if she slipped out.

'What were the two bearded wonders saying to upset you?'

Belle could have stamped a foot in her frustration. It would be Nick—without his women.

'Nothing at all,' she answered rather tautly. 'Why?'

'You looked a little ... cross, as you moved away from them,' he supplied, his blazing smile as shockingly beautiful as ever.

Belle's mouth tightened with resentment as she realised he must have been watching her just at the moments when she had been thinking about him.

'I can't remember now,' she lied nonchalantly and gave him a limpidly innocent look. 'How did you escape your dual escort?'

He understood the allusion at once. 'They were hardly keeping me prisoner,' he drawled.

'Of course not.' The smile Belle gave him was tight and hard. 'No woman can do that.'

The blue eyes narrowed contemplatively. 'What's the matter? Would you rather I still had my ... ah, escort? Is Schallau afraid we might find we've still got something going for us? I thought he seemed somewhat wary of me when I spoke to him a few minutes ago. It wasn't very clever of you to omit to tell him you'd been married, Belle. Naturally it would arouse his suspicions and make him wonder if a flame wasn't still flickering amid the ashes.'

'But there was never a fire, Nick,' she reminded him tonelessly.

'But he doesn't know that, does he?' Nick pointed out reasonably, but his smile was cynical. 'After all, most couples marry for reasons somewhat more solidly conventional than ours—or at least, they persuade themselves that that's the case. Would you like me to reassure him for you, let him know how slender the chances are of us ever getting it together again?'

Belle looked at him coldly, quite genuinely disliking him in that moment.

'No thanks, Nick, that shouldn't be necessary,' she managed distantly. 'I'm quite capable of telling him myself, should I deem it necessary.'

'Will he believe it, coming from you?'

'Oh, I think so.' She smiled delicately. 'Travis knows me well enough to know when I'm telling the truth, and I would be, wouldn't I? But I shouldn't think it will prove necessary. You and I won't be seeing that much of each other, will we?'

What she thought of as his professional expression appeared, implacable, unyielding, hardening the handsome face.

'I've told you, I need your help, Belle,' he said quietly.

'Travis or Terry or Marilyn would serve just as well. They all know Taiwan as well as I do, perhaps better.'

'London recommended you specifically.'

'Oh, God, you're forcing me to be honest! Nick, I know it's easy for you to ... to Be Civilised, as it's called, and to talk about—for old time's sake. But it isn't easy for me!' She had begun tempestuously, fully intending to shock him with the truth, but now she paused, seeing the wary, guarded look in his eyes and knowing that she could not risk either his pitying derision or the imposition on him of a burden of guilt, always supposing he possessed sensitivity enough to feel shame for what he had done to her. She went on in a more controlled tone, 'I was eighteen, Nick. That was my youth. That time between schooldays and true adult responsibility is precious—and so short it can be measured in months. I counted after I left you. Six whole months I wasted, agonising over you and our marriage because I was too young and too stupid to know any better. I know it was largely my own silly fault but, I can't help it, I still resent you.'

'I know. Would it help if I said I'm sorry, Belle?' Nick's face was dark and, for once, utterly devoid of humour. 'I have realised what I did, taking advantage of your obvious infatuation for my own rather selfish reasons and never pausing to consider the effect on you once your obsession had passed.'

'I don't want apologies, Nick, especially when, as I've said, I was partly to blame. I'm merely trying to explain why I don't want anything to do with you now. One of the others will have to help you. I don't like remembering how idiotically besotted I was.'

'I need you, Belle.' Nick spoke quietly.

She looked down momentarily, flushing. The times she had dreamed of hearing those words, and now they came, but in altogether the wrong context.

'Nick . . .' she began achingly.

His quick scintillating smile appeared, melting her. 'At least think it over for twenty-four hours; you haven't really had a chance to do so yet, have you? Have dinner with me tomorrow night and see how you feel about it then?'

'Damn you, Nick Rosney, why do you have to be so bloody irresistible?' Belle gave him a small, wry smile.

'Don't worry about it, darling girl.' His typically expansive gesture ended with his hand touching her shoulder, completing the destruction of her will-power. 'You're in no danger this time around. Tomorrow night, Belle? I'll pick you up at your office at, say, between seven and seven-thirty.'

He really was a self-centred bastard, she thought ruefully, loving him. How could she deny him anything?

'All right,' she yielded helplessly. 'But for tonight, I've had enough. I'm leaving. I'm not enjoying myself, and I have a heavy workload tomorrow. Another air force pilot has defected from mainland China and the press conference is tomorrow morning.'

'Can I see you home?'

'No, thank you. I'm a big girl now, Nick.'

'Not physically.' His laughter was abrupt as his eyes travelled over her figure once more and Belle turned away, hating herself for the warm deliquescent awareness his look evoked.

'Tomorrow, then.' Her voice was a thin thread of sound.

To her surprise, Nick was present at the air-base for the official interview with yet another of the pilots who had recently defected and been rewarded with a high-ranking commission in Taiwan's air force and a box of gold which Belle always thought rather a quaint touch.

Only approved members of the media had been invited to the short question and answer session, so it seemed that for once in his life, Nick was doing something approved of and authorised by the government of the country he happened to be in, and why not? He always presented a fair picture and Taiwan had little to hide or be ashamed of.

Belle's lips quirked as she stared at the back of his dark head. He would probably find it very tame going after the opposition and adversity he had faced in such diverse parts of the world as Eastern Europe, the Middle East, South and Central America.

'Who is he?' Sitting beside her, having come along as interpreter, Sue-Ching had followed the direction of her gaze.

'Nick Rosney,' Belle said and, because she would probably have to introduce them some time and Nick would mention it if she didn't, she added, 'My ex-husband.'

'You never said!' The small pretty Chinese girl was enchanted, her dark eyes sparkling with interest. 'I heard he was here to make a film about our country. Do you still speak?'

'Yes,' Belle sighed. 'In fact, he wants my help,

information, etcetera, so I suppose, if I decide to give it, that we'll be seeing quite a bit of him for a while. Although, come to think of it, you'd be a more appropriate person to aid him. It's your country and you speak both Mandarin and English fluently.'

'Ah, no, I am only an apprentice still,' Sue claimed modestly, her immaculately made-up little face glowing. 'I would be too shy. But Belle, do you think he would . . . Ah, no, he is too famous and busy a man to submit to interview with someone so junior.'

At twenty-one, Sue was humble but ambitious. She had taken an English degree at the local university where an American lecturer on contract had given her the Sue part of her name, and now in addition to working as Belle's assistant and interpreter, gaining experience for her own future journalistic career, she occasionally submitted her own freelance work to Taipei papers.

Belle laughed. 'Try him and see, love. I think you'll find him co-operative. Nick is very generous about regarding even the most junior reporter as a colleague of sorts, a fellow member of the media.' Her laughter died and the shadows darkened in her green eyes. 'I was eighteen when I went to interview him although, admittedly, I was standing in for someone else.'

'That is how you met?' Sue was intrigued.

'Yes, and I don't think our marriage touched him deeply enough to put him off being interviewed by young female reporters, so try your luck, Sue.' She paused, looking at her attractive assistant. 'Only, don't let him marry you.'

'Some chance,' Sue giggled, glancing at Nick again. 'He wouldn't look at me! Anyway, my fiancé might have something to say. But Belle, tell me about your marriage, or am I impertinent to ask?'

'No, but there's nothing to tell. It simply didn't work for various reasons.'

She was relieved when the pilot was escorted into the spacious interview room at that moment, since she was reluctant to list those reasons, even to Sue, who was probably the closest friend she had in Taipei with the exception of Travis Schallau.

After the session was over, Nick came across to them as the ranks of the press began to divide, gathering into groups or hurrying off to other assignments.

'Still all right for tonight?' he asked Belle rather perfunctorily. 'Who's this?'

'Sue—Nick Rosney,' Belle addressed her assistant who was blushing prettily under Nick's brilliant gaze and sensational smile. 'Nick, this is Chen Sue-Ching, my invaluable assistant and, as you may have noticed during the last half-hour, my interpreter. She also does the occasional piece of her own for local papers.'

'And I would be deeply honoured and most grateful if you would consent to let me put a few questions to you, Mr Rosney, sir,' Sue found the courage to venture formally and Belle felt sympathetic, realising the girl was holding her breath while she awaited his answer.

'It will be a pleasure,' Nick assured her easily, vivid blue eyes inspecting the Chinese girl's lovely figure. 'And there's no time like the present, so why don't you leave with me now and we can have an early lunch together somewhere? I'll leave the choice of venue to you.'

'Belle?' Sue was looking at her in an agony of supplication and, irritably jealous as she was beginning to feel, Belle forced herself to smile.

'Go ahead, Sue, I don't need you for the next couple of hours,' she assured her.

'Oh, thank you,' Sue breathed fervently.

'Let's go, then,' Nick suggested.

As Sue moved away, Belle murmured waspishly, 'One thing, Nick. She has got a fiancé. Try to remember that.'

He looked back at her blandly, assessing her figure this time, slender in a cream skirt and long, loose blouse worn with a thin double belt of pale leather. Then a gleam of wicked amusement appeared in his eyes.

'There's no need to warn me, darling girl. I never make the same mistake twice.'

Turning, he strode away and, seething with a resentment she knew was unreasonable and showed a not very nice side of her nature, Belle watched him catch up with the dainty Sue and put a protective hand to her slim, vulnerable back as he steered her through the crowds.

'Fast operator, that ex of yours,' someone commented and she swung round agrily to face Terry Whelan. 'And stylish too, dating little Suzie right under his ex-wife's eyes and never batting an eyelid, let alone raising a blush!'

'They're merely going to lunch,' Belle snapped. 'She wants to interview him.'

'Sorry I uttered!' Terry's grin faded as he stared at her. 'Hey! I really am sorry, Belle. I was assuming it had left you as untouched as it obviously has Nick Rosney, but I can see there's still something there where you're concerned. Poor old Travis! Share a taxi with me?'

'Oh, God,' she muttered hollowly, bending to retrieve her tiny tape-recorder and bag.

If even Terry thought Travis had a romantic interest in her, it was beginning to look as if she would have to face him and lay a few things on the line. The trouble was, she didn't want to lose his friendship, but she didn't want to become his lover either. It was all Nick's fault. This other thing wouldn't have surfaced if he hadn't arrived.

She had a busy day. There was her usual session with the government press office, an interview with two visiting Japanese businessmen who, even though they came from Tokyo with its renownedly vast population, confessed themselves terrified by Taipei's traffic, and then filing her reports for clients all around the world took up a great deal of time. She also had to visit a pottery factory for a feature for the Saturday evening supplement section of a paper at home, observing how steady little hands turned out work of miraculous delicacy, much of it based on the old, traditional Chinese designs. The painting fascinated her most, young artists copying by eye from vases that stood in front of them the tiny, delicate strokes, infinitely patient and careful.

'What happens if someone makes a mistake?' she questioned the young woman who was showing her around.

She beamed. 'Then they have created a new design.'

Belle laughed. It was a happy philosophy and typical of the thrifty, industrious nature of Taiwan's people. Nothing ever went to waste.

Between all these activities, she made time to return quickly to the shared apartment in the early afternoon to pick up something to wear that evening since Nick was fetching her from the office. She had no idea where he intended taking her, but she might as well dress up a bit since she had so few opportunities to do so.

Who was she kidding? Belle grinned ruefully to herself as she walked back to the office once more. She just wanted to look her best for Nick, that was all, fool that she was. Would she never learn?

Sue-Ching was back at her desk when she got in.

'How did it go?' Belle asked smilingly, hoping she sounded casual.

'Like a dream!' Sue was ecstatic. 'You were right, Belle, he is very generous. He just gave—so much! Except . . .' The piquant little face clouded. 'I mean as Nick Rosney, celebrity, he gave, but when it came to his personal life . . . Nothing! It's not that he refused to answer my questions or clammed up, but he would not be serious for one moment. Everything was a joke.'

'That's Nick,' Belle told her drily. 'One day I'll explain him to you, Sue-Ching, but not until you've submitted your piece. You wouldn't want your view of him to be influenced by me.'

'So it wasn't that I approached it in the wrong way?' Sue was anxious for reassurance.

'No, even the most experienced of us would have elicited an identical response,' Belle assured her. 'A private Nick Rosney doesn't exist.'

'I have an idea, Belle!' Relief made Sue brighten and her eyes grew mischievously thoughtful. 'Why don't I interview you as his ex-wife? A sort of second opinion?'

'I sincerely hope you're only joking, angel,' Belle laughed.

'Of course.'

'Thank God for that! Now, if you don't mind, I've some background research I want you to do at the university archives.'

Sue had returned a few hours later but had gone home by the time Nick called for Belle. She had changed in the cloakroom that served their floor in the building of rented offices, re-done her make-up and spent considerable time fiddling with her hair, once more prey to the beguiling memory of Nick's liking for it when it had been long and straight. Almost, now, she regretted it and she wondered bitterly what had happened to her pride. Nick's preferences should mean nothing to her; she wouldn't let them mean anything.

In the next moment, however, she caught herself relievedly recalling that he had said it suited her like this. Certainly it made her long-lashed eyes look huge—and a bit too vulnerable at times, she thought unhappily—and it emphasised the adult fining of her features, the hollows beneath her high cheekbones investing her with an almost hungry look that was softened by the delicate silky tendrils that framed her face, night dark wisps with a subtle glint of red here and there.

Her dress too was flattering, a simple strapless sheath of dark jade silk that made the green of her shadowy eyes even darker and hugged the slenderness of thighs, hips and waist and the firm lift of her small breasts above which her graceful shoulders and neck gleamed softly, smooth as the silk. Her only adornment was a pair of long jade earrings purchased locally at the Handicraft Promotion Centre, jade being in plentiful supply here.

She looked light years away from the girl Nick had married, she decided with some satisfaction. The guileless, slightly plump eighteen-year-old was gone forever; in her place a slim, soignée sophisticate. They were two different people—with only one thing in common, one thing that would never change.

'Quite stunning,' Nick commented with his quick dazzling smile when he arrived, surveying her.

'You look rather sensational yourself,' she responded lightly. 'I like the suit.'

In fact, he looked devastating. He so rarely wore suits but she had always liked him in one, liked the air of urbanity it gave him.

'I've found it an irritating bit of luggage but it's always a wise policy to take one along when visiting buttoned-up countries such as some on my present list. Sometimes the lack of one can prevent you getting to the man at the top.'

'For me it's easier. The only extra I take along for such occasions is a pair of stockings or some tights,' Belle laughed, thinking—God, it was a strain, Being Civilised.

'Ready to go?' he demanded with typical impatience.

'Yes. How are we going?'

'The team and I have hired several cars and vans for the duration of our visit. Let's move.'

As she walked through the door with Nick behind her, Belle remembered that she was required to give him an answer tonight. She was supposed to have spent last night and today deciding whether she was prepared to give him whatever help he wanted, but she hadn't really had time to do much serious thinking. In fact, she had largely forgotten the need for a decision although this dinner date had been constantly in her mind.

She had been looking forward to it, if somewhat nervously but she still didn't know what answer she was going to give him.

CHAPTER SIX

NICK took Belle to the Grand Hotel, outside the city, cursing the waywardness of the traffic although the fact that they drive on the right here presented no problems for someone as travelled as he was, and he seemed to have found his way about in an impressively short space of time.

'Your Sue-Ching recommended it as a favourite of yours,' he explained as they drove between the towering red pillars at the entrance.

'When someone else can afford to treat me,' she murmured drily.

'Is that a subtle warning that you don't intend going Dutch?'

'You're the one who called radio television's poor relation,' she reminded him laughingly.

'True. Why wouldn't you accept the allowance I wanted to make you, Belle?' he asked quietly as a uniformed attendant waved them into a parking place.

'Why should I have let you pay for what was equally my mistake?' she returned coolly. 'Marriage had neither robbed me of my ability to earn a living nor prevented me from doing so ... And there was no child to support.'

'Yes,' Nick agreed sardonically. 'It's just as well I didn't give in to you when you suddenly developed that crazy urge to start a family.'

It was not a good start to the evening. Belle hated the reminder. It had been one of the occasions on which Nick had openly accused her of immaturity, and knowing that the reasoning behind her desire, if anything so confused could be termed reasoning, had been not only immature but selfish and inconsiderate to the child they might have had didn't help. All the same, the thought of conceiving and bearing Nick's child could still turn her to jelly with its sweetness.

'Thank God you didn't,' she claimed fervently.

'It would have been the biggest mistake of all time,' he concurred, switching off the engine. 'But why so vehemently thankful, Belle? Is it because you've discovered that you are, at heart, a career woman?'

'Well, that, partly,' she confirmed out of pride. 'But additionally it would, as you've implied, have been quite, quite disastrous, not to mention cruel.'

'Cruel?' Nick repeated curiously. 'Cruel to whom?'

'To the child we would have had, had you let me have my way,' she explained carefully, hoping she was succeeding in concealing her pain. 'You were right at the time, Nick. My reasons for wanting a baby were all wrong. God! You were married to a child; you didn't need another in your life.'

'At least you had sufficient intelligence to know it must be a joint commitment and didn't take a unilateral decision to stop using your contraceptives as some women do,' he commented, and laughed abruptly. 'This is farcical. Here we sit, discussing a child we never had and never will have!'

'Crazy,' she agreed faintly, chilled by the ring of finality with which he invested the words.

'Let's go in. Shall we have a drink before we eat?'

The Grand Hotel was a magnificent example of traditional Chinese architecture, with vast spaces inside and more graceful pillars in that clear, beautiful red. Almost overwhelming in its luxury and opulent grandeur, predominantly red and gold, it would have graced any romantic tale out of Imperial China.

Nick reverted to impersonal subjects as they dined, and Belle was glad to follw his lead, even finding that she was enjoying herself. Nick always had been able to make her laugh with his irreverent wit, and some of his questions about Taiwan made her wonder just how long he would continue to have government approval. It didn't really worry her, however, not in a relatively humane country like this, and Nick wouldn't be Nick if he failed to delight in tilting at sacred cows. He was a born iconoclast.

Over coffee and liqueurs, however, he asked, 'How are your parents?'

'Very well, thanks. I receive a joint letter from them once a month. My father, needless to say, is immensely proud of my career.'

He grinned. 'But your mother would rather see you happily married with a couple of brats?'

'She has never grown out of being a romantic traditionalist,' Belle said indulgently, thinking rather sadly that she herself had been forced out of her own idealism, otherwise she might have gone on viewing life and love almost as rosily as her mother. 'And your parents, Nick? How are they?'

'I wouldn't know.' He shrugged. 'I haven't seen or been in touch with them for years.'

Belle could still feel faintly shocked by the gulf that yawned between him and the strange couple she had met in Bristol.

'Nick, they are your parents,' she couldn't resist saying gently. 'Don't you think they might feel a need to see you occasionally, especially now that they're getting older?'

'Don't be silly, dear girl,' he drawled, leaning back in his chair and regarding her with hard amusement. 'They've never needed me and they never will. What beats me is why two such self-contained people ever

had a child in the first place, or how they even came to
marry each other. I can still remember, as a child,
being told not to make an exhibition of myself and
how they'd put themselves out of reach if ever I tried
to get close—both figuratively and literally.'

Belle was silent, sipping her coffee. A child would
have counted such things as rejection. No wonder he
was incapable of loving now, if his parents had made
him ashamed of emotion. Any emotion he was still
able to feel was expended on the nameless masses
whose tragedies he revealed to the world; rarely on
individuals.

She recoiled in nervous alarm as Nick lifted a strong
but slender hand to the side of her face, and he looked
surprised.

'What's wrong? I was admiring your earrings.' He
lifted one dark pendant with the top of a slim finger
and let it drop again. 'Pretty. Jade? It suits you.
Finished? Shall we go then?'

'Yes . . . Yes, all right.' Belle could still find his
rapid digressions disconcerting.

She still hadn't given him an answer, she realised as
they walked outside, and he hadn't raised the subject
although he had asked her a great many questions
about Taiwan, with special reference to politics, the
economy, the religion of the people, a happy
commingling of Buddhism and Taoism, and the
traditional customs that had their roots in ancient
Cathay.

She didn't know what to do. One treacherous part
of her was tempted, so strongly, to grasp at the
opportunity to see as much of Nick as possible during
the coming weeks and thus feed the hunger that had
gnawed at her so relentlessly for five years, but in a
more rational frame of mind, she knew that to do so
would be fatal. There would be new pain to add to the

old and at the end, she would be left with a hunger far greater than that which she had already endured because, as she was discovering, her emotions had grown along with the expansion of her mind, part of the maturing process.

She had loved Nick at eighteen, desperately and frantically, adoring him, but now, on seeing him again, that love had become something quite mercilessly devouring, consuming her with its ferocity. The old love had caused her to suffer; this could destroy her.

The most sensible thing to do, and the only way to protect herself, she knew, would be to refuse to have anything more to do with him. She should recommend that he look to Travis or Terry for any information he needed . . . Not Sue or Marilyn, she thought, because they were women.

She blushed at discovering such a horrible dog-in-the-manger tendency in herself, and as if to atone for the disloyalty to the two girls, she said, 'Oh! I meant to say, Nick—thank-you for being so kind to Sue today. She was thrilled.'

'She made an appreciative audience,' he replied mockingly. 'And she's a lovely girl. How old is she?'

'Twenty-one.' Belle was beginning to wish she hadn't raised the subject although she was aware that her jealousy was pointless and unnecessary. Even the loveliest woman in the world wouldn't succeed in awaking any real emotion in Nick.

'Intelligent too,' he commented thoughtfully as they began the short drive back into the city.

'Yes, it can be embarrassing because she's actually much cleverer than I and yet she feels she had to defer to me.' Belle confided self-consciously.

'Why are you always on about how stupid you are, Belle?' Nick demanded irritably. 'You never lacked intelligence.'

The exasperated tone took her painfully back to the days of their marriage and she went on quickly, 'All the same, Nick, Sue-Ching would be the best person to supply you with information about Taiwan. It's her country, after all. I'm willing to lend her to you.'

'I thought of that,' he agreed mildly. 'In fact, I put out a few feelers over lunch today, but in the end I decided against it. She's completely objective about the rest of the world situation and will make a good journalist one day, but where the mainland China–Taiwan thing is concerned, she still needs to free herself of a certain amount of indoctrination. So, it will have to be you, Belle.'

'Will I get a credit?' she asked guilelessly and he laughed.

'Perhaps an acknowledgement, if that's what you want.'

'Will I get paid?'

'No, dear girl, you'll have to do it for love.'

'I assume you mean love in the tennis-playing sense?' she queried smoothly, secretly wondering how so many innocent little words and phrases could hurt so much, like small darts carrying an agonising poison that went on working in her system long after the initial sting had faded.

'Love meaning nothing,' Nick confirmed easily.

Of course, she thought bitterly. This wasn't personal; it was a professional matter. It wasn't as if he wanted her specifically. If Sue-Ching had proved the better bet, he would have used her. He simply wanted the best available, and she ought to be flattered.

Well, what the hell! She could be professional too, and it couldn't do her career's reputation any harm if it were known that she had been associated—

professionally!—with Nick Rosney. Why should she allow Travis or Terry to walk away with that sort of kudos?

'It's a deal,' she said softly.

'Thanks,' Nick answered casually as if he had been in no doubt about her decision.

Belle regretted it instantly. God knew how she was going to cope, but she couldn't retract the words now. If she tried, Nick might guess how she was feeling, and pride or something similar wouldn't stand for his pity, scorn or derision, the only reactions such self-betrayal was likely to provoke in him.

She was silent as Nick went into detail about some of the things he would be wanting to know or find out. They were things he and his team could have discovered for themselves, given time, but Nick was accustomed to working fast and she saw that a great deal of time could be saved by using someone with her knowledge of the country. She also realised that the feature he was planning was something excitingly different, an original investigative work that would embrace aspects and angles too often ignored in considering countries like Taiwan.

'Can you do it?' he asked as they approached the central city.

'Oh, yes,' she said confidently. 'I can start by giving you the notes I've made over the last year. If you'd like to drop me at my office I can give them to you now, and then I'll walk back to the apartment from there.'

'If you don't mind, I'd like you to come back to my hotel with me for a few minutes. I've got something I want to give you. Something—reminded me of it back there at the Grand Hotel,' he finished with strange constraint.

'Oh, what?' Belle was instantly intrigued.

'Wait and see.' Now she heard a smile in his attractive voice.

'Damn you, Nick, now you've made me curious,' she accused and he laughed but said nothing further.

In the foyer of the Ambassador, he retrieved his key from reception and turned to Belle: 'Just wait here a minute, will you? I have to get something out of the safe deposit.'

Whatever it was must have been small enough to fit in his pocket because he wasn't carrying anything when he rejoined her. She only knew it couldn't have been his passport because he always kept that on his person at all times, as a provision against having to get out of a country in a hurry, not to mention for purposes of identification should Nemesis ever overtake him.

Belle had often wondered, during the anxiety-fraught days of their marriage, what the odds were for war reporters. She had tried to comfort herself with other statistics; flying odds were one in thirteen flights per individual and Nick had flown hundreds of times—which had started her worrying about his flying so frequently and finding little consolation in yet another statistic which said more people died on the roads than in aircraft disasters.

She had tended, then, to resent his job, even while she understood it, but now she knew she would still have worried had he worked round the corner from his home with not even a road to cross. Cars could go out of control and mount pavements, people could suddenly go berserk with guns ... when you loved, you worried. It was part of the condition.

They took the elevator up to Nick's suite where he seemed in no hurry to hand her whatever it was he meant to give her.

'Drink?' he offered her, prowling with typical restlessness while she stood looking at him expectantly.

'No thanks, unless . . . Is there any coffee-milk?'

'You can look and see.' He indicated the mini-bar fridge.

Belle opened it and found what she sought. Most of the hotels stocked it; it was a delicious way of keeping up one's coffee intake in this hot climate and she had often unashamedly drunk various visitors' supplies when interviewing them in their suites.

'What is it?' She had sat down to insert the straw and had drunk half the small carton's contents before looking up to find Nick watching her with oddly brooding eyes. 'I mean . . . What was it you wanted to give me?'

'Oh, these.' He slid a hand into his pocket, extracting a small, soft leather case. He started to open it, but paused suddenly, looking at her, and Belle became aware of the cold, controlled anger that was emanating from him.

'Nick?' She put down the carton of coffee-milk next to her clutch bag.

'You know, Belle,' he went on almost conversationally, but his eyes were glittering, 'when you left me, it was because you'd grown up, grown out of your adulation, but you couldn't resist that last extremely childish gesture, could you? Here, take them. They're yours, they were given to you.'

He dropped the open leather case into her lap and Belle picked it up automatically, drawing a quick breath when she saw what was contained in the separate compartments.

'Nick . . .'

'I had them all professionally cleaned when I knew

I'd be seeing you again,' he said with a twisted smile.

Unable to speak, Belle looked down at her wedding and engagements rings, the matching emerald earrings, and the set of opals he had given her for her nineteenth birthday—or rather, the opals he had caused to be delivered to her—necklace, earrings and ring. They were truly beautiful, she realised now, Australian opals of the highest quality, each stone iridescent and with a soft fire in its heart, but at the time they had been a symbol of Nick's indifference, arriving professionally wrapped from the same establishment at which they had purchased their nuptial rings, and she had stared at them with a blazing, hurt anger before tugging off her rings, finding the emerald earrings and placing the lot in Nick's safe.

'What did you think you were proving by leaving them behind?' Nick said coldly. 'Anyway, you'd better have them back now. I've no use for them. Did you think I had?'

'Oh, I thought they might come in useful for future girlfriends,' she claimed flippantly, wondering how she ought to be handling this. 'The opals, anyway, were never worn.'

A light blazed in Nick's eyes but he merely drawled, 'I hope I've more style than to give my . . . ah, girlfriends, jewellery chosen for another woman . . . And that she was my ex-wife would be adding to the insult.'

'Well, they weren't exactly chosen for me,' she reminded him pointedly. 'Not by you, anyway.'

'You know there wasn't time, Belle,' Nick said rather wearily, shrugging out of his jacket and loosening his tie.

Belle swallowed, suddenly choked with emotion.

When he sounded like that, human, with his fragility on view, she no longer wanted to fight with him. Her youthful unreasonableness must have tried him sorely and she owed it to him to be adult now.

'You're right, Nick, it was childish of me, and if you really want me to have them back, then I accept.' She smiled very brightly. 'God, I must really have been unworldly back then, to walk away from these for the sake of a gesture. They'll come in very useful if ever I'm down and out. Thank you.'

'My pleasure,' Nick said suavely, seating himself on the arm of her chair, and his nearness caused her to feel faint and on the defensive once more. He put out a hand and lifted her wedding ring from its slotted compartment. 'I was especially surprised that you left this. Many divorced women still wear their wedding rings, just as they retain their married names, just to show they've been married.'

'Well, perhaps many divorced women are proud of having been married, however unsuccessfully.' Belle's tone was hostile. 'But I'm not, just as I'm sure you're not.'

She glanced at his left hand, lying relaxed on his thigh, and she grew very still. She must have seen it, last night and today; of course she had; but she hadn't really absorbed the significance of the continuing presence of the gold ring she had placed on his finger all those years ago.

Nick smiled sardonically. 'I may not be proud of it, but I'm not ashamed either.'

'Then you should be,' she snapped. 'We got married for such—silly reasons.'

'Silly, but not shameful.' He lifted his left hand and looked at his own ring. 'Now, this little item has come in useful with one or two subsequent girl-friends ignorant of the facts ... It prevents them from asking for more than I can give.'

And even when he did give marriage, he still didn't give very much, Belle reflected, sad and bitter, her eyes growing dark.

'You are appalling,' she said slowly and softly, with a sort of resigned affection, feeling wry tenderness for his very awfulness. He was so flawed, so empty, and so inexpressibly dear.

'Does it still fit?' he asked abruptly with one of his mercurial changes of mood and subject, picking up her left hand in his, his grasp tightening when she stiffened and tried to pull away.

'No, Nick, don't!' She didn't want to see and feel that ring on her finger again, but he was already sliding it on, and she wanted to weep suddenly for what she had never really had.

'No, too loose,' he murmured idly as the ring slipped down her finger and hung loosely.

He lifted her hand to his face, to his mouth, and Belle went rigid with rejection as she felt his lips move in the hollow of her palm, but when his tongue gently touched the smooth flesh, for just the most fleeting of moments, she felt the old familiar melting sensation begin and it was all she could do not to twist herself round and lose herself in his arms.

He was merely experimenting, looking for changes, she told herself coldly, trying to find the voice to stop him.

She looked up into his face and found his expression oddly intent, although the movement of his lips, trailing up her fingers and then down to the narrow frailty of her wrist remained languid, exploratory.

'Nick, I think you'd better stop,' she advised shakily.

'Why?' he asked lazily, smiling into her eyes.

'Oh, hell,' she muttered helplessly as a sweetly piercing sensual awareness shafted through her.

He would seduce her, for the sheer hell of it, just as he had once married her, too selfish to care about the damage to her emotions, too blind perhaps to even imagine it.

Nick moved abruptly, standing up swiftly and moving round in front of her, pulling her up out of the chair, and the leather case fell to the floor. Belle swayed and as their bodies touched, sheer naked desire for his possession scorched through her, making her gasp with its force and intensity. She had never wanted him quite like this before, instantly and violently.

Nick's hands and fingers moving on the bare skin of her back and shoulders seared her, although his touch was light. Helplessly, involuntarily, Belle moved closer to him and his hands separated, one going up to cradle her head, the other moving to the small of her back, steadying her.

'What else has changed, Belle?' he murmured obscurely. 'Let me find out.'

She thought she was going to faint when his mouth covered hers, and a small moaning sound came from the back of her throat as she felt the sensuous slide of his tongue, his kiss as erotic as the act of love it symbolised, deep and searching.

Oh, God, she hadn't been prepared for this! She had forgotten how to remain reserved and she had been without him, starving for his touch, too long for the art to be relearnt now. She was out of control already. She could have torn off her clothes then and there and offered herself to him instantly, right there on the carpet at their feet, so devouring was the merciless passion that flamed in her. There was a pounding ache in the lower part of her body, the fierce

pain of desire denied for too long, and already her hips
were moving spasmodically against him, mindlessly
signalling her need, her thighs weak and quivering,
eager to welcome him.

'Nick!' Her voice sounded harsh and strained, as he
drew back a little, sliding down the zip of her sheath
which slithered down to her hips.

His darkened eyes went to the dusky rose of her
congested nipples and then his hands were covering
her breasts and the hard, sensitised peaks seemed to
throb tenderly as they thrust against his palms.

His long sensitive fingers worked, massaging and
kneading the already swollen flesh, and Belle cried out
hoarsely, throwing back her head as wild, almost
excruciating desire and pleasure overcame her completely for a time.

Then, shamed, she realised that she was panting like
an animal while her fingers twined frenziedly in the
midnight darkness of his hair.

Nick moved one arm to form a bar across her back
as his mouth swooped to hers once more, but his other
hand continued its crushing palpation of one aching
breast with a faint violence she did not remember from
before.

But although her love and passion were deeper now
than five years ago, Belle was older and wiser. She
knew why he was doing this. He was on an easy
assignment, a holiday as he had said, and feeling
human, in Graham Thurlow's words. In the mood for
some sex, a little light lovemaking. And it would be
light, she knew, light and controlled, while she
suffered the humiliation of complete, wanton abandon
because her desire was so much greater than his, a
fiery, agonising wanting pulsating through all her
being.

It wasn't fair, she thought wildly, that he should

be the only man who could make her feel like this.

And why her, tonight? Perhaps Deborah Palmer had failed to deliver, or perhaps the identity of his partner didn't matter to him and he couldn't be bothered to seek Deborah out when he already had a woman nearer at hand. Even when he stirred, hard and swollen, against her, Belle knew it meant little. Probably any presentable woman would have that physical effect on him when he was in the mood and holding her tightly against the length of his body.

'Oh, you bloody, bloody man,' she protested huskily as his mouth moved down to the graceful line of her shoulder, lips and tongue stroking, kissing, sucking, teeth gently biting. 'No, Nick, we'd better stop now. I don't think this is a very good idea.'

'Why not?' He sounded amused. 'Let's go to bed, Belle.'

'What for?' she taunted bitterly. 'Old time's sake?'

'What's wrong with that? You want me.'

He had drawn back a little, his eyes going significantly to the taut fullness of her nipples, and Belle flushed.

'Of course I do,' she managed lightly, moving out of his reach. She even produced a smile. 'You are dead sexy as you damn well know, and very, very skilled, but . . .'

Only, it occurred to her as she pulled up her dress, something of the old finesse had been absent tonight and in its place had been an element of blindly compulsive quest. Perhaps he had been a long time without a woman. That was probably also the reason for his slight flush and the perspiration beading his brow and upper lip.

'But Schallau wouldn't like it?' Nick supplied.

'It's not that. But business and pleasure . . . They

don't go, Nick, and we now have a professional arrangement, don't we?' She smiled delicately, lifting a hand to smooth her hair, and the loose wedding ring **fell** off.

'How utterly symbolic,' Nick drawled, stooping to retrieve both it and the little leather case while Belle picked up her clutch bag.

'Very. May I use your bathroom?'

'Help yourself.'

She hated her reflection in the bathroom mirror, bright swollen lips devoid of lipstick, flushed cheeks and huge eyes, dark and glazed.

Order restored, she rejoined Nick. 'I'll leave now. If you don't mind, I think I'll see myself home.'

He held out the leather case. 'Take this with you.'

'Thank you. And thanks too for . . . an enjoyable evening.'

His smile was ironic. 'Don't forget those notes you promised me. Can you deliver them to me tomorrow morning? We'll be shooting an illustrative sequence at that temple I was telling you about.'

'All right. Goodnight, Nick.'

That bloody professionalism of his, she thought wryly as she left the suite. He was never really free of it, because it was his only reality; every other aspect of life was merely a game to him.

Then as she recognised a smartly suited young man getting into a lift, her own professionalism leapt to the fore and she set off in pursuit, since he happened to be the press liaison officer accompanying a joint delegation from the South African ministries of Foreign Affairs and Industry, Commerce and Tourism, in Taiwan to reaffirm links between the two countries.

By the time she reached the lifts, the doors had closed on him, but the door of the other opened as she was about to push the button and Carey Devane stepped out, her expression growing first indignant and then hostile when she saw Belle.

'Trying to get him back already?' she enquired maliciously, amethyst eyes hard and scornful. 'You haven't a hope. God! You should hear how he laughs over that marriage of yours. What a fiasco!'

Belle looked at her assessingly. 'I can imagine. You were right that time, Carey, I did end up with custard in my face, and it's not an experience I'd want to repeat. But perhaps you should issue a similar warning to Deborah Palmer? Hopefully, she'll have the wit to heed it.'

Judging by Carey's outraged gasp, the impulsively aimed shaft had found its mark, but Belle didn't pause to listen to the rejoinder, stepping smartly past her and into the lift.

She regretted her remarks almost at once. She and Carey were, in a sense, in the same position, and she supposed there was something admirable about the way the secretary had stayed on with Nick long after their affair was over. She knew she couldn't have endured a similar situation, but there were many ways of loving; hers was not the only way.

Belle finally cornered her quarry in one of the hotel's restaurants and they discussed the interview she wanted, wrangling briefly over his insistence that she first submit a list of questions for approval.

The matter settled more or less satisfactorily, she chatted him up a bit and bought him a drink. The two Japanese businessmen she had interviewed earlier were also staying at the Ambassador—it provided a special Japanese breakfast—and having taken a liking to Belle, they came over to say hullo when they saw her and happily accepted her invitation to join her and the liaison man.

Belle knew what she was doing, sitting here

drinking with three strangers. She was avoiding going home. Her flatmates were likely to be either out or asleep and she didn't want to be alone because, alone, she would start thinking, and remembering, and then she would cry.

She thought ironically that she seemed to have contracted Nick's need to have a crowd constantly about him. She had often wondered what daemons could haunt such a careless, laughing character to make him hate being alone, except immediately after lovemaking when he seemed to require solitude, and had finally decided that he simply sought people because he needed diversion in order to be able to bear the boredom of his leisure hours.

She was facing the restaurant's entrance so she couldn't help seeing him when he came in, with Deborah Palmer, looking regally ravishing in a simple white dress, at his side. Belle glanced at her watch and felt anguished resentment welling up inside her.

Less than twenty-five minutes ago, he had been making love to her, inviting her to come to bed with him. Now here he was with another woman. He hadn't lost much time in settling for the alternative option, she reflected acidly, stoney-faced under the mocking grin her ex-husband cast in her direction. She had been right; the identity of his partner didn't matter to him. He was just in the mood to share his bed with someone, anyone, just as long as they were female, functional and reasonably attractive.

She wondered how far Deborah Palmer was aware of the truth, but perhaps she preferred it this way, a casual encounter that didn't infringe on her liberty. She had to be a fairly dedicated career woman to have climbed to a point where she was assisting Nick Rosney with the chance of finishing the series on her own, so she probably valued her independence.

Anyway, she looked as if she could take care of herself.

Belle finished her drink hurriedly and excused herself. She would rather go home and cry alone for Nick than sit here watching him with another woman.

CHAPTER SEVEN

WAN moonlight filtered through the canopy of cloud that hung over Taipei at this time of year, finding the chink in the meagre curtains and shafting gently on to the opals that lay on the table beside the bed.

Belle lay on her side, staring at them. Her bed was hard. Most beds in Taiwan were hard, even in luxury hotels catering for visitors from all over the globe, because they were supposed to be healthy and someone had had the kindly idea of benefiting the health of visitors to this emerald isle of the Pacific in the same way that the collective Taiwanese health was benefited.

Belle's eyes and throat felt raw because, inevitably, she had wept.

She had returned to the apartment to find only Marilyn McMillan at home, sitting hunched over a glass of whisky pinched from the supply Travis kept hidden in the broom cupboard and thought no one else knew about since it was rare for anyone to find time to actually take out a broom or squeegee.

From Marilyn's terse explanation, Belle had gathered that she and Terry Whelan had once again quarrelled violently.

'I don't think we'll ever work it out,' she had concluded miserably, and with considerable fellow-feeling, Belle had washed a glass, lined it with ice-cubes and further depleted Travis's precious private stock.

'At least we'll sleep well,' she commented later as they said good night and went to their rooms, but she hadn't fallen asleep and she didn't suppose Marilyn had either.

The opals had been the last straw, she thought now, her tears still damp on her face. They had hardened her resolve to leave Nick. Her cases had already been packed when they had arrived, and Ransom, Nick's servant, had been hovering anxiously, knowing what she intended and deploring it, but too conscious of his position to attempt to dissuade her.

The deterioration of their marriage had begun during the honeymoon period, but in those days she had still been capable of hoping against hope. During that first separation, Belle had been wildly optimistic, promising herself that on Nick's return she would allow no further doubts to shadow her happiness. She would have faith, and never lose sight of the fact that, of his own free will, Nick had married her.

She had had approximately twelve hours' notice of his impending return and had obtained leave from the magazine. Compassionate leave, she had jokingly called it, explaining that their honeymoon had been interrupted, but she suspected it was only because her husband was Nick Rosney that it had been granted to her.

She had watched him on television during his absence. It had been a way of keeping in touch with him—but a stranger came home to her, a man blanched of colour save for his vivid eyes, his shadowed face all planes and angles, hollowed out, black and grey and white, barely coherent, so intense was his fatigue.

His kiss of greeting had been perfunctory, a mere brushing of his lips against her cheek. Belle had been nervous to begin with, feeling like an intruder in his home, but gradually, over a special dinner she and

Ransom had devised together, she had seen him begin
to unwind. He even cracked a few jokes.

When they had gone to bed, Nick had switched out
the light and turned to take her in his arms, and relief
had flowed through her. He was her husband still.

But after a short while she had become aware that
his embrace was wholly passive. He was doing nothing
to develop it; he was simply lying there, holding her,
his eyes shut, his face against her smooth hair. She had
stirred tentatively, experimentally, wondering if he
was waiting for her to take the initiative and arouse
him, but her shyly erotic movements had elicited no
response beyond a faint sigh.

The trouble was, she herself had been aroused by
the contact with his warm, hard-muscled body. Her
need for his possession had grown almost intolerable
during his absence and now the wanting had become a
fierce ache within her and her movements had grown
involuntary, something she was unable to help as
mounting frustration touched them with an element of
frenzy.

'For God's sake, Belle, lie still and stop wriggling
about like that,' Nick had snapped irritably after a few
moments. 'I don't want to make love to you; I just
want to hold you and go to sleep.'

'But I do! I . . . do want to make love,' she had
informed him rather huskily, wounded by his words.

'Then you'll just have to want.' His voice had been
hard.

'I . . . I've missed you so, Nick,' she had protested
yearningly. 'I've been so worried, and I've . . . I've
wanted you. Please . . .'

'God! Spare me the emotional speeches,' he had
adjured impatiently. 'Now, are you going to behave or
must I go and sleep in one of the other rooms?'

With an ungracious and incomprehensible murmur,

Belle had indicated compliance, sighing as she had forced her body to be still, loth to lose him altogether.

Later, when he slept and had somehow moved until her breasts served as a pillow for his head, his face turned against their softness, Belle still lay staring into the darkness. She still longed for him and the sweet weight on her aching breasts was doing nothing to ameliorate the pain of desire, but as she had lifted a hand to touch his hair, stroking it adorningly, she had suddenly been overwhelmed by a rush of tenderness for him.

He wasn't a god after all, merely a man, a human being, full of flaws and frailties, and she had been selfish and inconsiderate, thinking only of herself and her own needs.

Naturally Nick's needs were presently different to hers. He had been covering a difficult and dangerous situation, and he had travelled thousands of miles. He was probably too tired to feel he could make their coming together a worthwhile experience for either of them.

In the morning, when he was rested and refreshed, or else tomorrow night . . . Optimism rose and Belle's lips curved in love and anticipation. Eventually, contented because she thought she understood, she too slept, her hand still lying lovingly against her husband's dark hair.

But morning had brought little change. Nick slept until after ten o'clock, and Belle had been up for more than a couple of hours when he had appeared, as she had showered and dressed when she had heard Ransom moving about the house.

Nick had remained at home all day and once again Belle found him a stranger. He had been aloof and unfriendly for the most part, although occasionally he chatted to her in the old, inconsequential way, even succeeding in making her laugh. But in between those times he had showed her just how moody he could be, lapsing into dark, brooding silences, or displaying flashes of temper, especially when she had rather pathetically tried to sweet-talk him into a more amenable frame of mind.

'For God's sake, Belle, leave me alone!' he had exploded finally in the evening when she had mixed drinks for both of them and naïvely invited him to join her on the couch and tell her what was wrong. 'You're carrying on as if I were some bloody baby, to be wheedled and coaxed into good behaviour. I know I'm behaving badly, damn it, but you'll just have to bear with me. I've already forced myself into an alien rôle to accommodate you, but that's as much as you're getting from me. I can't do any more.'

The words had chilled Belle, but she had been too afraid, and still too much in awe of him, to demand an explanation.

Nevertheless, she had been seething with resentment and frustration when Nick had come to bed that night—and absolutely determined that he would make love to her.

'No!' His voice had been sharp as he drew back when she pressed her warm mouth to the hardness of his in response to the arm he flung across her. 'I told you last night, Belle, I'm not ready to make love to you.'

'That was last night,' she had protested somewhat violently, afraid of weeping. 'You're rested now, Nick, so why can't you?'

'I just don't want to,' he had stated brutally, sitting up.

'And what about what I want?' Belle had demanded furiously, also sitting up. 'I want you to make love to me, Nick. You're my husband. I have the right to . . . to——'

'To demand your conjugal rights?' Nick's laughter had contained no humour. 'Demand away, Belle. You're not getting. I think I'll sleep next door.'

He had left the bed, and the room, without bothering to turn on a light, as sure of his way in the dark as a cat, and Belle had been left to cry herself to sleep.

If only she could have been sure of his love, she had thought sadly, then she might have been able to accept all this, Nick's contrariness and temperamental rudeness, with a degree of equanimity because she would have had the one prize, to be cherished above all, to sustain her, keeping her strong and patient.

But he had given her so pitifully few proofs of his love, barely any indication at all, really, save for marrying her, and her doubts were multiplying as Nick seemed to grow further and further away from her, becoming a remote stranger, barely aware of her unless she irritated him.

He had gone out the next day to report to the network bosses and see the accounts department about his expenses, so Belle put in a day at the magazine and had got home before him.

At least he was looking more like himself again, she had thought achingly when he arrived and poured drinks for them both in the large comfortable lounge. There was colour in his face once more, a little less tension, and his dark blue eyes as well as his lips smiled when he talked to her in a typically light vein.

He was talking more too, she had realised, getting back to the man who was compelled to fill every silence with talk and laughter. All the same, she didn't feel inclined to forgive him yet; he had hurt and humiliated her, she thought resentfully, and he probably didn't even realise it, so self-absorbed was he, and particularly so since his return, so completely caught up in his black mood that he was unable to consider anyone else's feelings.

Her resentment had grown when Nick had succeeded in making her giggle helplessly over his description of the running battle he had fought with a straitlaced dragon in Accounts.

Sobering, she had changed the subject abruptly, enquiring with stiff aggression, 'I suppose you're going to refuse to make love to me again tonight?'

Nick had seemed momentarily startled before giving her a long, coolly appraising look. 'Probably,' he had agreed indifferently.

She had smiled coldly. 'Then may I suggest that we at least do something together?'

'Like what?' He had sounded wary.

'Going out.' The coldness had melted and she had sounded eager. 'Let's go somewhere for dinner, Nick. We could go somewhere there's dancing, or if you really can't face that, then even just a movie would do. A meal and a movie?'

'Sorry, Belle, I just don't feel like going out,' Nick had said flatly, his expression impassive, and she had got the impression that he didn't really feel any regret at all.

'You used to feel like it every single bloody night before we got married,' she had reminded him.

'Well, I don't now,' he had retorted impatiently. Then he had sighed and smiled ruefully. 'Do I seem terribly unreasonable? Listen, Belle, let me explain——'

'You don't have to explain anything. I wouldn't want you forcing yourself into an alien rôle.' She had repeated his words of twenty-four hours previously with a bitter inflection. 'And you would be, wouldn't you, because you never voluntarily explain anything?'

'Belle——'

'I don't want to hear!' she had flared. 'Anyway, I already know the explanation. The joke has stopped being funny, hasn't it, Nick? You don't want to be seen out with a moronic lump like me.'

'Don't be so bloody childish, Belle,' he had advised icily.

'Well, what else do you expect?' Her voice had shaken with anger as she had stood up. 'I'm only eighteen, Nick, I left school last year! I admit it, I'm childish, I'm immature, I'm an imbecile. You knew all this when you married me, so what else can you expect?'

He had nodded wryly. 'I knew all that and, fool that I am, I still went ahead and married you.'

Now there was genuine regret to be heard in his voice and Belle had felt as if he had stabbed her with a knife. With a choking sound and stumbling slightly, she had run out of the room. At the door, she had glanced at him out of the corner of her eye and her humiliation had been complete. Nick had picked up the newspaper he had brought home with him and was becoming engrossed in the main story. He had forgotten her already.

She had gone into the study because it was the nearest, slamming the door and crying like the child he had accused her of being, loudly and furiously, but with a touch of real desolation too, because she was convinced that Nick had just broken her heart.

A little later, when she hadn't been able to keep it up any longer, she had hauled her typewriter on to the desk and began to type up some notes for a magazine assignment, pounding the keys angrily, swearing at mistakes and still sobbing occasionally because she had kept remembering Nick's words and the hurt was growing instead of subsiding.

Their marriage was a failure. Nick regretted it and

she had no idea how to handle the situation. He was right, she was too childish for him, too young—and too stupid.

She had still been typing a long time later when she heard Nick enter the room.

'Didn't you hear Ransom?' he had enquired mildly, standing behind her. 'Dinner.'

Belle hadn't looked round or stopped typing, although her fingers had become slow and clumsy. 'I'm not hungry. I'm busy anyway,' she had said sullenly.

'Busy, or sulking?'

She had flushed. 'That's the sort of childish behaviour you'd expect of me, isn't it?'

'Come and eat, Belle,' he had urged rather wearily.

'Later. I've told you, I'm busy.' She stopped typing.

'I'd like you to eat with me.' Nick's voice had suddenly contained the old charming note that usually had the power to make her melt, but this time Belle hadn't softened.

'Well, tough,' she had taunted. 'I'd have liked you to eat with me every night week after week just recently, but you weren't here. This time I'm the one with work to do, so you'll just have to do without me for a couple of hours.'

'And see how it feels?' He had laughed a little. 'Are you sure you're not sulking, Belle?'

'Leave me alone, Nick.' To her mortification, her voice had cracked.

Instead, he had moved round to her side and cupped a hand gently beneath her chin, raising her averted face. For a few seconds he had looked blankly at her tear-stained face, mascara streaks lining the course of her tears.

He had smiled rather crookedly. 'I'm sorry, love,' he had said lightly.

'Go away, Nick!' At the end of her tether, Belle's voice had been edging towards hysteria.

Nick had nodded curtly, removing his hand and silently leaving the room.

She had expelled a shuddering sigh. No, he wasn't sorry at all, she decided, almost hating him at that moment, and to make matters worse, he was more or less right: she supposed it was sulking when, however hungry she was, she had no intention of joining him in the light, elegant dining-room—and she was starving!

She had started typing once more, but less than five minutes had passed when Nick had re-entered the room with a tray which he set down after clearing a space on the desk, grinning mockingly at her resentfully enquiring look.

'You see, I think I'm right and you *are* sulking,' he had told her. 'An indulgent husband, am I not? Knowing how you like your food——'

'I already know I'm fat,' she had flared touchily and he had made an exasperated sound.

'Don't be ridiculous, Belle, you are not fat,' Nick had stated emphatically. Then he had smiled again, his most sensationally charming smile. 'But I'd hate you to go hungry, my darling.'

'Oh, Nick,' she had sighed resignedly because she had to smile back. His smiles and laughter were always so warming, however little they really meant.

He had moved nearer to her, laying his hand on her head and passing it over the smooth shining length of her hair. 'Poor baby, you're so emotional.'

Baby, she had reflected with some chagrin, but she had said nothing, simply leaning against him and yielding herself to the pleasure of that tenderly stroking hand because she had no wish to prolong the quarrel and this was the kindest Nick had been to her since his return to England.

In future, she had promised herself, she would be less emotional.

She had thought he might change his mind and make love to her that night, but he hadn't even come to the master bedroom, and another night of sleepless frustration had been enough to revive a certain amount of resentment.

Nick had remained in the house the following morning so Belle stayed at home too, since she actually had a full working week's leave and she had gone in the day before. Not that he seemed to require her company, she had thought petulantly, and went into the study to go through the file of press-cuttings about a dress designer on whom her superior was planning a feature.

She had been constantly aware of Nick's presence in the house, however, because he had been restless, prowling about, with something of the devil in him. He had kept telephoning people from the various telephones scattered about the house, using the study one to call a firm of art dealers and demand that they send someone round—at once—to look at a painting he had just that minute decided he didn't like, and in between the calls and his peregrinations, she had heard him talking to Ransom, being utterly outrageous, trying to get a rise out of the impassive servant and actually succeeding on a couple of occasions.

Full of hell, she had reflected with wry indulgence. It sounded suspiciously like boredom that was driving him. Then suddenly she hadn't been able to hear him any more and, laughing at herself for being like the mother who only worries if her brimstone child is quiet, she had yielded to the temptation to go and look for him.

She had found him upstairs in the master bedroom. He had been standing in the middle of the room staring moodily at the wide bed, so deep in his thoughts that he hadn't even heard her come in. Somehow she had known he was thinking about her, about making love to her. She hadn't known why she was so convinced; it hadn't been conceit or wishful thinking; she had just known it with absolute certainty, and something in his expression, an odd, brooding regret, had brought a new, appalling possibility into her mind.

'Nick?' She had touched his arm and he had flinched, turning dark, disturbed eyes on her.

'What do you want?' Nick's voice had been sharp and strained.

'Nick, what is it?' Belle had whispered anguishedly. She had gestured towards the bed. 'Darling, if . . . if you can't anymore, for some reason, then it's all right, really it is. I won't ask you again. Only, I wish you had told me.'

'Oh, but I can, dearest girl,' he had drawled, composed once more, and amused. 'At least, I assume you're asking me if I've suddenly become impotent. I could have made love to you at any time I chose since my return, believe me. Only, I didn't choose.'

'Why not? Why didn't you choose?' Belle had hated that pleading note in her voice, but she couldn't help herself. 'Please tell me, Nick, I need to know!'

He had drawn away, looking at her with something approaching dislike. 'Why must you always make such a production out of everything, Belle? Sex is a very pleasant pastime, an enjoyable distraction for an hour so, but it hardly merits being built into a great emotional issue, does it? I'm going out; I'll see you later.'

He had gone before she could frame a reply, and she sank helplessly on to the end of the bed, burying her face in her hands, Pleasant, enjoyable! Did he mean sex was that way with her, because she didn't really excite him, or was that all it amounted to for him, irrespective of his partner because he was incapable of the loving that made sex the ultimate, complete experience of fulfilment, spiritual and physical?

A minute later she had heard the roar of his terrifyingly powerful car as he had left.

When he had returned he behaved as if no moments of discord had ever existed between them, the old, careless, laughing Nick, the man with whom she had fallen so irreversibly in love.

'You said last night that you wanted to go out, so I'm complying, like the doting husband I am, twenty-four hours late, it's true, but to atone for the delay I'm prepared to put up with dancing,' he had informed her, hugging her.

Perhaps it was still going to be all right, Belle had thought with a lightening of her heart, but now her optimism had been cautious, touched with a wariness that seemed well-justified when, to her disappointment, she had discovered that he had booked a table for six, inviting two other couples to join them, including Graham Thurlow and his current girlfriend.

Nick had finally made love to her that night, still with that cool self-restraint he had exercised during their brief honeymoon, and Belle had drawn blood by biting fiercely into her lower lip in her endeavour to temper her passion to a level that matched his and keep from crying out in wild, enraptured abandon to the controlled beat of his possession.

Afterwards, he had gone away, as she had known he would, and she had lain tearless but anguished in the darkness, putting away dreams and looking at reality. He had made love to her with an easy indifference, just as if it were some sort of routine exercise or task, neither pleasant nor unpleasant simply necessary, like shaving.

She had wondered why he had even bothered, but perhaps he had pitied her and felt he owed it to her, having married her; or perhaps he had simply been in the mood for sex and since he was still trying to be faithful to her, he had made use of her availability even though she didn't really attract him.

Or perhaps he had simply been proving to her that he wasn't impotent.

Whatever it was, she had to accept the fact that Nick didn't love her.

Only she hadn't been able to accept it. To do so would have meant a sort of dying and Belle hadn't been able to face that. So she had sought other proofs, challenging him, especially when the call came for him to fly away again, because if only he could have made some sort of sacrifice for her sake, it would have provided her with a measure of hope to live on.

But Nick had yielded nothing. That first return set the pattern for all the others. When he returned from either a long trip or a short one, he would want simply to hold her the first night, leaving her angrily if she tried to seduce him, and she had soon become too self-conscious and humiliated to try, and it was always some days before he would make love to her.

There had been tears on Belle's part, and tantrums, but Nick's occasional displays of temperament had been more spectacular than hers, and also more rare. Usually his attitude towards her had been one of weary exasperation and she had realised with horror that she was becoming sullen and nagging. This was not the sort of burden to lay on a man who came home exhausted and drained from the horrors of war and disaster, she had known, and yet she hadn't been able to help herself, and his irritable impatience had only

seemed to goad her into making more frantic
challenges as she had sought desperately for some hint
that he loved her—and received none.

His absences had been worse in a way, because then
she had worried. The time he had been in Iran had
been the worst. He had become a fugitive, wanted by
the ruling power and with a ghastly fate awaiting him
should he be caught, and he had been forced to go
underground. For a time nothing had been heard of
him, and Belle had learnt what hell was then. The
optimistic kindness of the television people and the
strong warning issued by the Foreign Office to those
who sought him failed to comfort her, and when the
news had finally come that he would be returning
safely, she had wept all over her colleagues at the
magazine.

In an excess of fervent relief and gratitude, Belle
had vowed that henceforth she would be a model wife,
the sort of unemotional and undemanding wife a man
like Nick Rosney needed, never asking for more than
he could give, merely grateful for that which he did
offer.

Like most such resolutions, it had been aborted
almost at once, when Nick had immediately and
irritably denounced her coming to meet him at the
airport as emotional posturing.

The danger he had been in haunted Belle for weeks.
If he hadn't come back, she would have been left with
nothing, with no part of him remaining for her to
cherish. Once again, she had broached the subject of
his abandoning the dangerous aspect of his career, but
now there was a difference. Always before, she had
been challenging him, demanding a sacrifice she didn't
really want simply because he had failed to give her
other more important proofs of his love; this time she
was begging him out of her fear of losing him, for a

time quite genuinely wanting that sacrifice, whatever it might cost him in terms of frustration.

And she had watched his face grow hard and remote, and listened again to his accusations of childishness.

'Nick!' In the middle of an exchange of recriminations, the idea had occurred to her. 'Nick, why don't we have a baby? Our marriage is a mess, you've just admitted it and I agree, but a baby might mend it, and . . . and . . .'

And she would still have a part of him, if ever anything did happen to take him away from her forever. The mere idea of having Nick's child made her weak with emotion.

Nick's face had grown so dark that she had thought she was about to witness one of his shows of temper, but after a few seconds, he had said coldly, 'Don't you think you're a little immature for motherhood?'

'You thought I was mature enough for marriage,' she had reminded him petulantly. 'What's the difference?'

'I knew you were young, but I didn't realise just how immature you were.'

'Perhaps having a baby would make me more mature!'

'I suppose the two of you would grow up together?' Nick had taunted. 'What the hell sort of idea is that, Belle? It would be madness to bring a child into the sort of marriage we've got. Forget it.'

'Do you regret our marriage, Nick?' she had asked in a small voice and wished she hadn't, knowing what the answer must be.

His lips had twisted. 'It has hardly been a success, has it? Yes, my dear, I rather think I do regret it.'

'Why did you marry me anyway?' she had

whispered, her eyes huge and almost black with anguish in her suddenly pale face.

The look he gave her had been blank, indifferent, as he had shrugged. 'Impulse, I suppose. A crazy, regrettable impulse.'

That was it then. She had had her answer, quite conclusively. There would be no proofs of love forthcoming and she might as well stop seeking them. She ought to leave at once. Yet, masochistically, she had stayed on, torturing herself, waiting for Nick to ask her to leave.

Strangely, having destroyed her with the truth, he had become kinder, as if he knew how she was suffering and was doing what he could to make up for his inability to love her, but kindness hadn't been able to solace her. She had come to the conclusion that he was incapable of loving anyone at all, and it was the knowledge that all her hoping and praying had been expended so pointlessly that crucified her, along with the humiliating awareness that she had lacked the physical attributes and skill to arouse even his sexual appetite to any great heights of passion. He had used her, married her on impulse as he had admitted, simply because he had wanted to amuse himself by shocking or surprising his friends, and she ought to hate him.

Only, she had still loved him, her hollow, careless, mercurial husband, and so she had stayed to face the bitter end.

It came when her nineteenth birthday had been approaching and they had been married for approximately six months. Nick had seemed to take a special, indulgent interest in her birthday, asking her some weeks before the event what she would like to do to celebrate it, but she had been unable to think of anything beyond dining out.

'You choose somewhere and surprise me,' she had suggested. 'Only, Nick, just this once . . . Can it be just you and me, and no one else?'

'I'm flattered,' he had mocked gently. 'All right, love, I'll see if I can come up with something special.'

Despite her sadness, Belle had found herself looking forward to her birthday. Nick had told her he had booked something, but enjoyed refusing to tell her where and what when she asked him, reminding her that she had wanted to be surprised.

Then, less than a week before the day, the call had come.

'But what about my birthday?' she had asked in a small voice when he had told her that he had to be at Heathrow within the next three hours.

Nick had looked at her blankly and she had realised that all personal considerations had slipped his mind the moment there was work for him to do.

'I'm sorry, Belle.' He had been flat-voiced and perfunctory. 'I have to go.'

'But you promised——'

'For God's sake, girl, surely you had the intelligence to realise it was a qualified promise, contingent to my being free at the time? I didn't think I had to warn you of possible disappointment, the way one does a child. I thought you accepted it, but then, you are still only a child, aren't you?' He had paused, seeing the tears that had filled her eyes, and had dropped a hand to her shoulder, but Belle had flinched away from the contact.

'Nick, please, just this once, couldn't you——'

'No! Look, love, when I come back——'

'How do you know you'll come back?' she had asked shakily.

'Of course I will,' he had claimed with arrogant impatience. 'When I come back, we'll go out and——'

'If you're not here for my birthday, then I won't be here when you come back, Nick,' Belle had stated, the knowledge only just having come to her. It was time to go. She couldn't take any more, and she didn't even really want any sacrifice from him because it still wouldn't mean he loved her.

Nick had stared at her, then laughed with apparently genuine amusement. 'I wondered how long it would be before that particular solution occurred to you. Congratulations, Belle, it looks as if you're growing up at last. So you're leaving me? Well, then, there's no more to be said, is there?'

With dawning, horrified comprehension, Belle had watched him stride away. Nick hadn't asked her to leave, because he had been waiting for her to make the decision to go. That way, he need bear no guilt for the ending of their marriage because it would be her action that terminated it. God, he must have thought her slow, and stupid, and thick-skinned!

Humiliated, she had forced herself to face him one more time, when he went out to his car a little later, knowing it was probably the last time she would see him in the flesh.

'Goodbye, Belle,' Nick had said and looked at her expectantly.

She knew what he was waiting for. They had become a ritual spoken at their partings, the words she had used when he had been called away from their honeymoon, and she had never omitted to say them, however resentful she was of his departure, telling him to take care, to mind how he went and come back to her.

This time, however, she had remained stoney-faced, secretly wondering if he had developed a supersitition about the words, regarding them as some sort of talisman. He would never admit it, though; he would never ask her to say them.

After a few moments, he had shrugged and got into the car. Belle had gone inside as he drove away, sinking to her knees in the hall and crying violently, moaning as she had rocked back and forth in an anguished paroxysm of grief, uncaring that Ransom might hear her. It was all done, all gone . . .

She had taken several days over her packing, and she had known her resolve to go hadn't yet hardened. She had still been waiting, for something, anything, to make her stay. Just a call from Nick asking her, please, to be there when he got back would have sufficed to turn her from her intention at that stage, but all that had come was the set of opals and they were the one thing that could harden her purpose.

She had looked at them, knowing Nick had probably 'phoned the order to the jeweller from the airport, telling him to send the best available. There was no card in his writing, nothing personal.

She had known then, from her sudden surge of anger, that she really must go. Her heart was still lost, or rather, in Nick's careless keeping, but she had found her pride again.

CHAPTER EIGHT

FIVE years later, reliving it all during a hot sleepless night in Taipei, Belle could acknowledge that she had behaved very badly, and the fact that she had been young, hurt and uncertain was poor excuse.

She could only thank God, for both their sakes, that Nick had never loved her. Had he done so, her stupidity, her wilful lack of understanding, could have hurt him badly, if it hadn't first killed his love.

But he hadn't loved her to begin with and so she was spared a burden of guilt she knew she would find intolerable.

Nevertheless, she was oppressed by a sense of shame. She didn't suppose Nick had deserved any better of her, and yet she wished now that she had given him better. He might have been unable to love, and equally incapable of true burning physical passion where she was concerned, but he might have learnt to be comfortable with her. Her most selfish behaviour had been during those brief periods immediately following his returns from various war-torn or disaster-stricken countries. He had needed someone quiet and comfortable to come home to, she thought now, with a better grasp of the temporary sickness that ailed him then, a sort of weary Weltschmerz, only stronger, and instead all she had offered him was a self-centred display of petulant challenge.

'Oh, Nick,' she whispered aloud, regretfully, turning on to her back once more as the first faint light of dawn began to steal into the room, pallid and somewhat dulled by the eternal clouds of summer.

If he had wronged her by marrying her as he had, on an impulse that had nothing to do with her save that he had needed a prop with which to make his joke and she had been stupidly, willingly available, then she had made him pay for it throughout the six months of their marriage because, God knew, he must have been irritated beyond endurance at times, she thought, reviewing the childish folly of those days.

Yet he had been surprisingly patient, she conceded with the wisdom of hindsight. He could have hurt her with far more deliberate intent than he had done in retaliation for the perpetual annoyance she had brought into his life and his home. She supposed it had been out of his awareness that he had wronged her that he had shown her such generous indulgence.

Poor Nick, trapped by his own boredom in a marriage that was a constant irritation, his wife a nagging child who didn't even attract him.

Belle laughed a little for the sheer tragi-comic folly of it all, a wan sound in the silent room, but her eyes were filling with tears again.

She must show him in the weeks to come just how reasonable and adult she could be, she thought. Her pride demanded it, but she also thought Nick would like to know how she had grown up. He would appreciate it.

The trouble was, she still loved him, and what had occurred in his hotel suite a few hours ago had reawakened her old passionate need for Nick. Belle had been shocked to discover how deep and extensive her feelings were now. Both love and desire were stronger, fierce unwavering flames that scorched her. She was grateful that her mind, too, was stronger, because otherwise she would have been devoured, destroyed, and she had no intention of suffering over Nick Rosney again—not ever again, and especially not now when the suffering would be worse than before because the loving was so much more intense.

She had always known herself, her heart and her mind, but now she knew Nick, knew his lacks and limitations. Never again would she believe that a proposal of marriage or, for that matter, an invitation to share his bed was his way of saying he loved her. He didn't, and she knew better than to hope otherwise. Hope was what had humiliated her all those years ago, keeping her hanging on in there when Nick had only been impatient for her to see the light and go.

Sighing, she sat up and got out of bed, early as it was. It was too hot to lie there, even with the air-conditioning turned up to cold, and too uncomfortable being alone with her thoughts, the memory of the way she had failed Nick a constant accusation. Somehow his lack of love for her couldn't nullify that failure—it mattered terribly even though he had failed her in another simpler way.

She went into the kitchen, switched on the coffee percolator and bit rather cautiously into a solitary Copenhagen she found in the bread-bin since she had no idea how old it was. Their housekeeping was not of the highest order, she reflected, wondering if she could find time to do some shopping during the day. Travis and Terry seldom bothered, leaving it all rather unfairly to Marilyn and herself, who had equally crowded days, although the men were easygoing about contributing financially.

She surveyed the day ahead while she showered, dressed, did her make-up and dried her hair. She had to take those notes to Nick—and face him with a serene smile, pretending he meant nothing to her, pretending last night was so unimportant that she had forgotten it . . .

Apart from the routine things, she had a couple of

special stories to pursue, and the South African interview had been tentatively scheduled for tonight. Well, she would fit Nick in, between challenging the Bureau of Commodity Inspection with complaints about quality from countries to which Taiwan exported, and finding a medical researcher who might be able to explain the high incidence of liver cancer among the male population here.

It would be interesting to see Nick at work, she told herself firmly. She wondered if he and Deborah Palmer had spent the night together . . .

'Oh, hell!' she exclaimed violently, disgusted with herself because it was none of her business.

'What's wrong?' Travis laughed, opening the door.

'Me!' she declared vehemently, closing her handbag and giving him a wobbly smile. 'I'm all wrong, Travis.'

'Now I'd have said you were all right—and rather ravishing,' he added gallantly, his look appreciative as it rested on her slender thighs and hips encased in khaki-green Ché pants, the broad waistband with its two slim leather belts making her waist look tiny beneath the loose, plain cream silk shirt she had chosen. 'Belle, can I have a word?'

She regarded him rather nervously. 'Just one, Travis, or many words?'

'Well, a few,' he offered with a smile that seemed rather forced. 'I've been kidding myself, haven't I?'

'Travis——'

'I'm not accusing, or blaming, or criticising,' he went on, seeing her wary, hunted look. 'I'm just asking for final confirmation before I . . . Well, before I accept that a rather pretty dream of mine is only that and will never be reality.'

Belle's sigh was a compound of regret and relief. 'I'm sorry, love.'

'Yes.' Travis also sighed. 'I think I knew the moment you walked in here the other day and saw him.'

'I really am sorry,' she repeated sadly. 'Because it's all so utterly futile. I wish ... That's why I'm all wrong, you see. The world is full of wonderful, sensitive men like you who ... And all I can think of is that ... that empty, emotionless ex-husband of mine. It's going to be that way for the rest of my life and I don't want it to be, Travis, I don't want it to be!'

'Hey! Now, don't cry, honey.' He came and put an arm about her suddenly shaking shoulders. 'Especially not when you've evidently taken so much time and trouble over your make-up! You're seeing him today, I guess.'

She nodded, keeping her lips compressed as she smiled because tears still threatened. 'Unless I chicken out and send Chen Sue-Ching,' she whispered chokily after a minute. 'Only I don't suppose I will because, I've got such a horrible nature, I'm jealous of every other woman he looks at, and he thinks Sue is attractive.'

'Tell yourself you're protecting her. You know him, she doesn't,' Travis advised with a gentle laugh and Belle also laughed.

She felt slightly better as she walked to the office. At least Travis understood, and he had been very nice about it, not aggressive at all. It was just a pity, a tragedy really, that none of them was happy just now, she loving Nick, Travis loving her, and Marilyn and Terry engrossed in their private and painful conflict. Then there was Carey Devane. She couldn't be very happy either. She wondered if Deborah Palmer was happy ...

Nick, now ... He was probably quite content, since

personal matters never touched him, and Belle wondered if she should regard him as fortunate, or terribly impoverished. In a way, she supposed, he was crippled, handicapped by his inability to love. It must be like having a part of you missing ... although such an amputation might be preferable to loving the way she did, hopelessly and idiotically, rarely free of the pain of it.

So much for the vanity which had made her take trouble over her make-up that morning, Belle was thinking a couple of hours later, one of a slow-moving throng of drenched pedestrians, walking with heads and shoulders bent against the great soft sheets of warm rain that were falling out of the clouds. Taiwan was not part of the monsoon belt, rain being perennial, and Belle had long since given up carrying an umbrella since the streets were too crowded for such an encumbrance, and she had noticed that the local population utilised umbrellas more for protection from the sun than from the rain. She never found walking in the rain uncomfortable, although it did little to ease the heat and humidity at this time of year, and the sun was still to be seen, a silver ball of fire behind the running clouds.

It had stopped by the time she reached the temple. The clouds had thinned to gauzy shreds, and Belle felt sticky instead of soaked once more, although her hair was still damp and the thin silk shirt clung to her, outlining every curve and indentation of her upper body.

The colourful temple to Buddha was quiet, the worshippers going about their business, the smell of incense heavy on the still, humid air. Immediately behind it, in the fashion prevailing in most Buddhist nations, stood the darker temple of the Goddess of Mercy and it was here that Nick Rosney and a small crew, including Deborah Palmer and Graham Thurlow, were filming.

'Belle.' Nick came over to where she stood watching when there was a break, and she felt slightly embarrassed as his eyes rested briefly on her shirt where it was still plastered against her firm breasts, the dusky red of her nipples very evident.

'The notes,' she said hurriedly, hating the husky note in her voice and unable to meet his eyes. 'Slightly damp round the edges, I'm afraid. I got caught in the rain.'

'I noticed. It suits you,' he told her wickedly, his eyes glinting, full of devilry, and she flushed.

'Nick?' Deborah Palmer, in white trousers and shirt worn with a scarlet belt and sandals, had followed him, casting Belle a sharply interested glance. 'I think Graham wants you.'

'I'll be with him in a minute. Don't go away, Belle, I want to talk to you. Incidentally, did you get to meet Deborah, my assistant, the other night? Deb, this is Belle Tyler, my ex-wife, but she has a greater claim to fame than just that, these days. She's the voice we so often hear over breakfast or sundowners in English-speaking countries.'

Breakfasts they shared? Belle watched him stroll away, thin but muscular in jeans and a white shirt, with something of a constriction in her throat because, oddly, he had sounded almost proud of her. Then she turned to smile tentatively at Deborah Palmer, inwardly hating her.

'I've been curious about you,' the older woman admitted candidly. 'I have to hand it to you. Nick Rosney is quite fatally attractive and his charm is even more deadly, but I'd think twice about taking him on as a husband. He must be hell to live with on a permanent basis and I'm not surprised it didn't work out for you. All the same. I think you were very brave.'

Belle had stiffened as she began, but meeting that clear, calm grey gaze, she could detect no hint of mockery. Deborah was complimenting her quite sincerely, it seemed.

'It wasn't brave,' she denied with a self-conscious smile. 'It was just the stupid, overweening confidence of youth.'

'In other words, you'd know better today?'

'That's for sure.' Belle hoped she didn't sound too embittered. She gave Deborah a direct look. 'Do you need the reassurance?'

'No, I don't,' Deborah responded composedly. 'Oh yes, like everyone else, I crave Nick Rosney—quite badly at times—and we've shared some mutually enjoyable hours in the past, although not on this trip, and that includes the weeks we've just spent filming in and around Seoul. But marriage or any sort of permanent relationship isn't for me. My career has just started to take off and I need to concentrate on that.'

They should suit each other perfectly then, Belle reflected acidly, disliking her again.

'Do you enjoy working with him?' she enquired politely.

'Yes, but he doesn't enjoy working with me,' Deborah laughed. 'You see, I love this sort of project, it's what I want to do all the time, but Nick wants to be where the real, violent action is.'

'Yes,' Belle sighed resignedly and Deborah gave her a comprehending look.

'Yes,' she repeated. 'If that's the way you feel, you're better out of it and so is Nick. Excuse me, I'm wanted.'

Nervously, Belle wondered what Nick wanted to talk to her about, but when he returned to her, it seemed that all he was interested in today was the project and the help she could give him, and she felt torn between relief and disappointment.

There was so much he wanted to know and to discuss, and she was kept busy in the days that followed. In fact, she thought wryly, he was something of a slavedriver, demanding an incredibly high output from everyone around him, but she supposed it was fair enough, since he himself put in longer hours than anyone else.

She was forced to delegate much of her own routine work to Sue-Ching who appreciated the opportunity to gain experience, but even so she began to feel slightly stretched, especially when a major story broke, so special that she didn't want to delegate it. She personally undertook to dig through the surrounding rumour and conjecture and get to the bare but startling bones of the matter, a Japanese cargo vessel having had a hole blown in her deck while passing between a region of the coast off mainland China and one of the small garrisoned islands belinging to Taiwan from which, respectively, Communists and Nationalists periodically shelled each other, although the exchanges were supposed to have become mere token displays of hostility as, these days, both sides tended mostly to fire blanks or propaganda leaflets.

But the Japanese captain's story seemed to contradict this and, much to Belle's disgust, he had headed straight for Hong Kong, so in between making a nuisance of herself with the Taiwanese military chiefs, she was forced to spend hours on the telephone, tracking down her various sources in Hong Kong, including another stringer who kindly arranged to put her in touch with the Japanese captain.

Meanwhile, Nick was conducting high-powered interviews with top-level government members as well as with the little man and woman in the street, going into their homes and questioning them about all manner of things, often borrowing Chen Sue-Ching to interpret for him, and Belle was aware that her assistant suffered a series of shocks at some of the abrasive, typically Nick Rosney questions he put, and was beginning to look at her country with eyes that saw more than just its many virtues.

The team were also filming background sequences, to be edited into the serious stuff as illustrations of the Taiwanese way of life, the emerald beauty of the little country and its determined prosperity. Belle suspected Nick found this aspect less enthralling than the gathering of hard issue material, but she enjoyed watching him at work and, since he frequently required her to be on hand to settle something that was in doubt, she had the opportunity to do so quite often.

They filmed the marble magnificence of the Chiang Kai-shek memorial, and a long sequence at a Chinese nightclub-style theatre where traditional magic and acrobatics were a counterpoint to gorgeous girls in slinky Western dresses, singing Western and Japanese songs, meant to illustrate that while one foot might remain in ancient Cathay, the other was firmly planted in the twentieth century. Nick also obtained special permission to film briefly in the New Chinese Palace Museum, one of Belle's favourite places, containing the world's most priceless, precious collection of Oriental works, some over four thousand years old, which had formerly been housed in Peking's Imperial Palace, exquisite pottery, ivory, jade, coral and lacquer-work.

Belle enjoyed observing the feature taking shape, appreciating the skill and originality Nick brought to what could have been just an ordinary travelogue-type documentary, but she was also becoming desperately unhappy. Seeing Nick almost every day was a form of purgatory, when he was so horribly, charmingly impersonal and she had to pretend to be the same.

Ruefully, she became aware that he was using her mind with far more passion than he had ever used her body, and she hated it. She didn't want to be his unofficial colleague, she didn't want even his professional respect! The only thing she wanted from him, and had always wanted, was the one thing he was incapable of giving to anyone.

She was even forced to see him when no meeting had been arranged, she thought miserably and somewhat exaggeratedly one morning, encountering him leaving the offices of the national censors just as she was arriving to ask for a list of cuts made to a certain controversial American film due for release in local cinemas.

'Ah, no, Nick!' she laughed as he stopped. 'Who are you taking on now? I'd have expected to find you being thrown out bodily.'

He grinned. 'I'm bigger than they are, but you're right, they're not too pleased with me. They didn't like some of the questions I asked them.'

Belle shook her head wryly. Censorship was strict in Taiwan and she had been amused, on obtaining entry to a banquet given for the South African delegation a few nights previously, to hear two young men, a Taiwanese and a South African, vying fiercely with each other, each attempting to prove that censorship was more severe in his own country, the Taiwanese gaining an edge by claiming that movies even had their endings changed here.

'They'll probably cut your film when it's shown here,' she warned lightly.

Nick shrugged. 'It's not really meant for Taiwanese consumption, but to introduce viewers elsewhere to a country about which too little is known.' He paused, blue eyes travelling over her slim body in the softly clinging buttercup dress and finally coming to rest on her tense, hollowed-out face. 'You're looking tired, Belle, all eyes.'

'Well, you're a bit of a slavedriver, aren't you?' she retorted tartly, touchy about any negative comment on her appearance when it came from him, because she still had a silly longing to be beautiful in his eyes.

'Am I? Has it been so bad?' Nick seemed surprised. Then he smiled, the old scintillating, meaningless smile. 'Never mind, Belle, I'll give you dinner again some time as a reward.'

It was a moment of weakness for Belle. 'You'd better make it soon, Nick, or something is sure to prevent it, the way it happened with my nineteenth birthday.'

His eyes went blank and empty for a fleeting moment, but then he laughed a little. 'What about tonight, then? Where shall I fetch you—your office? Between seven-thirty and eight?'

'Fine,' she agreed brightly, wondering rather wildly why she had done it. 'See you then.'

'Belle?' Nick was frowning as she started to move away.

'Yes?' She paused.

'Was it really so important, that birthday of yours?' he asked thoughtfully. 'I mean, young as you were, it was nineteen, not nine.'

Belle flushed. 'No. I suppose . . . it was an excuse I grasped. I think . . . I knew I had to go, you see.'

'And you chose that as your reason.' Nick laughed sardonically. 'It's ironic when you think of it, isn't it? You had grown up sufficiently to realise, finally, that you had to get out and yet you chose such a juvenile excuse. You didn't really need one, dear girl.'

'I know that now,' she agreed painfully, turning away because she was afraid of betraying herself. 'See you tonight, Nick.'

There were tears on her cheeks as she left, forgetting her appointment with the censors for the time being and presently finding herself wandering through some pretty parkland, landscaped in the traditional neatly pretty, small-scale Chinese way that bore a marked similarity to Japanese gardening.

She honestly didn't think she could take much more and it was beginning to feel as if she would never be happy again. She wondered if she had ever, for an hour or a moment, been truly happy since her wedding night. Now unhappiness was an active thing, tearing at her, weakening the fibre of her very soul. She had thought five years of missing Nick was bad, but this situation was infinitely worse, seeing him daily and being forced to acknowledge his complete indifference to her.

She had it confirmed once more that night when Nick kept the conversation entirely on impersonal subjects over the meal they shared. He took her to what the Chinese called a Mongolian barbecue, the upstairs restaurant open to the night air along one side. It was a novel way of eating because you selected your own meats, salads and sauces from a vast array, piling them all into one bowl and then watching them being cooked at a very high heat in a matter of seconds, the cook's movements swift and deft as he twisted and turned the mass about.

Nick talked, and Belle smiled and listened and laughed, and occasionally contributed something, and all the while she was crying inside. He had been her husband; now he was a stranger. He had even said it himself, to her flatmates—she had never really known him.

But when they stood up to leave, Nick's smile faded as he looked at her. 'Will you come back to the hotel with me for a while, Belle?' he asked curtly.

She arched her fine shapely eyebrows. 'More jewellery?' she enquired flippantly and he laughed rather abruptly.

'Don't worry, I won't try to mix business and pleasure this time,' he advised her smoothly, vivid eyes skimming over her figure, every slender curve revealed by the saffron dress which was held up by tiny sequinned shoulder-straps and was so slim-fitting that there was a pleated slit at the back to enable her to walk comfortably. 'Unless, of course, you want me to make love to you? No, it's just that I'm enjoying your company, Belle, and I'd like to go on doing so. It's still early ... We could have a drink or two, and continue talking.'

Belle lifted a graceful shoulder.. 'All right,' she allowed, lips quirking, and he nodded.

She averted her face as they left the restaurant, her smile growing tenderly indulgent. The truth was that, typically, he didn't want to be alone, only he couldn't say so. Well, she would go back and help him fill his emptiness and its haunting accompanying silence for as long as he wished, she thought warmly, strangely stirred by the prospect of being able to give him something he truly wanted for once, even if it was only her company and she knew that any other presence would have served equally well.

And at least he seemed content with her company alone these days and didn't seek the crowds he usually craved, she reflected ironically as he escorted her directly to his suite rather than scouring the hotel's restaurants for the additional company of his crew, some of whom were sure to be about.

He no longer felt guilty about her, she supposed

bleakly, and that was why he could feel comfortable with her—a colleague now, no longer a wronged, emotional wife.

Nick was in a good mood now, with plenty to say for himself. He could tell an entertaining story and Belle couldn't help laughing, but gradually an inner uneasiness was beginning to disturb her.

It had been a mistake to come to his suite because she was prey to the disconcerting memory of what had occurred last time she had been here. She sat listening to him, watching him pacing and prowling, flinging himself into a chair, leaping up again, gesturing in that way he had, and all the time she was being distracted by the recollection of his mouth on hers, his hands on her breasts.

It was becoming intolerable and the worst of it was that Nick wasn't feeling it, too. She was sitting here wanting him, deliquescent with desire, heavy-limbed with the lassitude of a sexual hunger that was becoming pain, and there he was, telling his stories, making jokes, all unaware of her aching frustration!

'I don't think you're listening to me!' Nick accused. He had stopped in front of her and Belle raised heavy-lidded eyes to look up at him, flushing when she saw his dawning comprehension.

Unspeaking, he examined her through his long eyelashes, a half-smile playing about his beautiful mouth. 'You do want me to make love to you, don't you?' he challenged softly eventually.

'Damn you, Nick,' Belle protested jerkily. 'Why do you have to be so attractive to me still?'

He laughed, reaching down for her hands and pulling her to her feet. 'Why not?' he mused thoughtfully. 'You're all grown up now, old enough to satisfy your physical needs without guilt and too old to make an emotional issue out of a sexual encounter. It can harm no one.'

He needn't know, she thought miserably, too deep in desire to resist, He needn't know how much of an emotional encounter it would be for her, nor the harm it would do, especially if he still made love to her with the old restraint. She needed him too badly to deny herself, every nerve-ending shrieking for his possession, her blood surging and clamant for the feel of his flesh on hers, his body in hers, and her pulses were racing.

'Take me to bed, Nick,' she whispered, knowing she was a weak and foolish woman but unable to help herself, even if she was destroyed afterwards.

'Yes.' He smiled brilliantly.

As he led her into the bedroom, she wondered if he was doing this out of a dispassionate kindness because she so obviously wanted him, a sort of pitying token atonement for things past, or whether he was simply in the mood for sex and she was available—more than available, she was willing, desperate, to go to bed with him.

The reason didn't really matter though, she knew with a weary hopelessness. She had to go through with it, that was all. It was the only way to ease the terrible tension that had been building up in her over the last few days.

She needn't see him again afterwards. She could crawl away and die somewhere, along with her pride.

Nick undressed her gently and divested himself of all his own clothes too before pulling back the covers of the bed. He took her shuddering form in his arms and she clung to him convulsively as, locked together thus, they sank on to the firm bed.

'Kiss me,' she begged languidly.

'Yes.' A faint sighing laugh escaped him. 'It has been a long time, Belle.'

Too long, she thought wildly as his lips nudged hers apart. Five long aching years of emptiness, of nothing, while he had been amusing himself with other women, Carey and Deborah, and there was precious little consolation to be had from the knowledge that they had probably meant no more to him than she had.

Nick's kisses were languorous, and controlled, as she had known they must be, but also deep and searching, awaking a throbbing response that made her writhe against him, her arms clamped vice-like about his neck and shoulders.

Still that reserve . . . And his eyes were wary, she realised as he raised his head, enabling her to look up into his face, as if he didn't quite trust her.

'What is it?' she questioned him breathlessly.

'What?' He even sounded suspicious.

'You seem . . . cautious.'

Nick's laugh was uneven. 'It's not infatuation now, is it?'

'No.' It never had been.

'Just sex? Lovely sex,' he murmured, smiling crookedly.

'Yes,' she lied.

He looked down the length of her. 'You have a beautiful body,' he murmured. 'It was always lovely, but now it's beautiful.'

Her head moved against the pillows in sad, dismissive negation. He didn't have to say these things, tell these lies. Not for her, but she knew how he liked to fill a silence with light meaningless words.

'You're the beautiful one,' she whispered achingly.

His body was long and hard, sleek and golden-brown, the cloud of dark hair on his chest arrowing downwards, and she touched it, stroked it, tentatively, and then lovingly, her fingers remembering.

'Belle.' He leaned over her.

'Nick!'

She arched, offering him her aching breasts and as his warm, moist mouth opened over one swollen nipple, a harsh strangled cry came from deep in her throat and her hands went to his head, fingers tangling convulsively in his hair which had a blue-black sheen in the light coming from beside the bed.

The erotic stimulation of his tongue, stroking so seductively, and the caressing downward movement of his hands on her body drove out all thought. She was spinning dizzily in a hot dark place where nothing existed save passion; she was floating and yet heavy, congested with desire.

She moaned deeply as his hand came to the place where she waited for him, wanting him.

'Let me touch you too, Nick.'

'Not yet. The light?' he questioned, lips moving against the pulsing hardness of each nipple in turn, those twin erections betraying her need of him.

'Put it out,' she said. At least then he wouldn't see her humiliated submission. She was ready to receive him already, frantic for him, wanting to pull him into her, and he ... he was still in control. Nothing had changed.

She welcomed the sudden darkness. Nick moved and now his lips followed the course of his hands and she whimpered like some small animal as she felt the rasp of his jaw and the caress of his lips on the silken length of her inner thigh, the sensuality of his kisses filling her with a piercing sweetness. Her blood felt like hot thick honey in her veins, her flesh was molten, sensitive to his every touch, and she simply didn't have bones any more.

He moved up over her again and she wound her arms and legs about his, her head thrashing from side to side on the pillows. His skin was slippery with sweat, he was shaking slightly and, to her surprise, he was also gasping. The sound excited Belle and she began to touch him, with feverish caresses, her hands seeking the hard throbbing evidence of his arousal, the vital, vibrant power that would conquer her and ease her and pleasure her—and ultimately shame her, she supposed sadly.

The shrill ringing of the telephone beside the bed was a shocking intrusion, but they were both so conditioned in obedience to that particular summons that they released each other instantly, Nick moving to sit on the edge of the bed as he answered it.

Belle lay on her back with an arm flung over her eyes, feeling sanity return as she listened to the terse phrases Nick was speaking into the receiver. Then she sat up, reaching round him to locate the light switch. She got up and began to dress.

Once again, the call had come. It would always be this way.

CHAPTER NINE

NICK rang off and looked at Belle rather warily as she slipped her feet into her high-heeled sandals.

'I'm sorry,' he muttered fretfully. 'It had to happen now, didn't it? I have to leave at once.'

'It's all right.' She didn't really know what to say.

'No tantrums?' he mocked, smiling slightly.

'Well, hardly. Even as your wife, I didn't have the right,' she admitted coolly, closing her mind to the male beauty of his body as he stood up.

'All the same, it has never happened at quite such an inconvenient moment before,' he mused, going to the cupboard for a robe and putting it on.

'It's probably just as well. It would have been a mistake, Nick ... You and me, I mean,' Belle concluded embarrassedly.

'Oh, yes. Business and pleasure?'

'That, and ... I've mentioned this before. I know it's unreasonable and I'm sorry, but I still can't help resenting you for my messed up youth.' It was the nearest she could come to the truth.

'It's not so unreasonable, Belle,' Nick said rather flatly. 'I took quite deliberate advantage of your rather obvious crush on me without considering the possible effect on you. That wasn't very nice or kind of me. In fact, it was probably rather cruel.'

She swallowed, uncertain of how to respond, and changed the subject. 'Is it something bad, Nick? Dangerous?'

'No, just vile. You've probably heard the rumours about refugees being cast adrift again as soon as they arrive without being permitted to set foot on land? A brief investigative report is all that's required, and I happen to be in the region—it's only two hours away by air. There's a cameraman waiting for me, so Deborah can carry on here with Graham. Can you see yourself home, love? I have to leave just about at once, but I've got to brief them first.'

'Of course.'

'You've got money for a taxi?'

'I'll walk. That's one of the advantages of a low crime rate. I feel safer at midnight in Taipei's darkest street than I did in broad daylight in any of the other places I've been in. I'll be on my way right now.'

'Yes. Goodnight, Belle.' He followed her into the lounge part of the suite and she paused.

'Goodbye. Take care, Nick.' She stopped self-consciously, realising what she had said, then shrugged mentally. What the hell, she might as well finish it. 'Mind how you go.'

'And?' Nick was smiling, remembering.

Belle laughed shakily. 'Well, I don't know. Will you be coming back, Nick?'

'Oh, yes, this thing should only take a few days, so I'll be back.' He paused, a speculative gleam in his eyes as they held hers. 'But not to you, I gather? A mistake, you said.'

'Yes, it wouldn't be . . . wise.' Her voice was faint and subdued, almost with a stifled quality, because the truth was oppressing her, suffocating her. They would never be lovers again because it would destroy her to have his lack of love reaffirmed even one more time and she had no intention of being destroyed. She had a whole life to live still and the only way it was going to be bearable was if she was diligent in sheltering herself from further pain.

'You're probably right,' Nick was agreeing easily,

heedless of the damage he inflicted by placing a hand on her shoulder and dropping a casual kiss on her smooth cheek. 'Goodbye, Belle.'

She was glad of the respite his absence would afford her, she told herself forcefully as she walked home, stopping to buy some fruit for her breakfast in the night market, and trying rather desperately to ignore the fact that her real gladness stemmed from the knowledge that he would be returning and ... she would see him again.

She seemed to have no sense of self-preservation, she thought angrily, her self-disgust growing as she reviewed the way she had behaved tonight. She would have given herself to Nick without a thought for the unhappiness and shame that would follow, and he ... He would have accepted what she offered, he would have taken her as a favour to her, out of kindness, simply because doing so couldn't harm or inconvenience him, and it probably appealed to his sense of humour too.

She could only thank God that Nick was too insensitive, too lacking in imagination, to guess why she should still want him after all these years.

A respite, she had thought, but it was no such thing. She thought of Nick constantly in the days that followed, fantasising about his return with a wild, wayward romanticism and knowing herself for a fool.

Even had she not been caught in the thrall of her devouring, pointless love for Nick Rosney, it would have been difficult to put him out of her mind. Deborah and the crew kept in touch, using her knowledge and Sue-Ching's bilingualism, but that wasn't all. The visitors from England had been drawn into the circle which constituted Belle's own social life in Taiwan, the gang of Taipei-based media people, an international, gregarious assembly of reporters for papers, magazines, and radio and television networks around the world.

They were all at a party given by an Australian journalist both Belle and Terry Whelan had known in their Sydney/Canberra days when she learnt of Nick's impending return. The party had only really got underway towards eleven; it was around midnight when members of the television team began to trickle in, and Belle was both amused and relieved to notice Travis making a beeline for Deborah Palmer. She didn't think she had broken his heart, and even if she had, he was too well-balanced and self-respecting to let it be a blight on his life forever.

It was Carey Devane who brought news of Nick, taking malicious trouble to ensure that Belle could hear when she said, 'I heard from Nick this evening. There has been a bit of a delay but he expects to reach Taipei sometime during the course of tonight. I expect he'll come on here.'

Deborah Palmer withdrew her attention from Travis to give her a look of dislike. 'Yes, he probably will because I left him a note telling him where I'd be,' she stressed.

Carey looked put out. 'So did I,' she stated sulkily.

Belle turned away, wondering what was happening to her sense of humour, because she couldn't even find their possessiveness amusing. Instead, all she could think of was that Nick would hardly be in the mood for partying when he returned.

Graham Thurlow caught her eye, and apparently his thoughts were following the same trend because he shrugged and said quietly, 'I shouldn't think Nick will feel much like a party tonight.'

'Yes, but he'll still pitch, rather than be alone,' Belle uttered her thoughts aloud, seriously and rather sadly.

Graham regarded her thoughtfully. 'Why the hell

did you ever leave him when you understand him so well, Belle? These other women haven't got a clue.'

'Ah, but I didn't have a clue either, back in those days—or rather, I did,' she added honestly. 'There was part of me which understood Nick's idiosyncracies, but I used to irritate him by wanting him to be different.'

'It sounds as if you'd accept them now?' Graham guessed shrewdly.

'It's a hypothetical point, but yes, I think I would,' she conceded gravely, knowing that then and now she would have accepted anything, if only Nick could have loved her.

'You still love him, don't you?' Graham's smile was sympathetic.

'I think just about everyone has realised that, except Nick,' Belle laughed ruefully, a sad little sound.

'He does tend to be rather blind about personal, emotional matters,' Graham allowed.

'Well, don't try to open his eyes, will you, Graham?' she requested, suddenly anxious. 'He has left me with so little else, so at least let me keep my pride. His pity would humiliate me.'

'Of course,' he assured her gently. 'Telling him the truth would be a pointless exercise when it can benefit neither of you.'

And if even Graham, who was probably Nick's closest friend, knew that, then there wasn't even the merest iota of hope left to cling to, Belle acknowledged bleakly.

'Thanks, Graham,' she murmured wearily and ambiguously.

'But, Belle, if you love him and he does pitch tonight, you'll get him out of here before the need to be sociable drives him to one of his explosions of temperament,' Graham suggested. 'They may be spectacular, but perfectly innocent and well-meaning people get blown up simply because their minds are a little too slow or silly for Nick's liking, and I suspect he always regrets it afterwards and finds himself even harder to live with, since he's not a cruel man when he's free from stress.'

Belle sighed. 'I would, Graham, only I don't have the right and, anyway, if it boils down to a choice between someone else getting blown up or my getting hurt again ... I don't think I can take any more pain,' she concluded in a voice that had sunk to a whisper.

'And what about Nick?' he prompted, making her feel selfish.

'Oh, I don't know,' she sighed again. 'I'll see what he's like when he arrives ... If he does. He may have picked up someone to allow himself to be unsociable without being completely alone. After all, he'll never experience any difficulty in pulling a woman.'

He didn't even have to do anything to arouse most women's interest, she reflected drily, and as the hours passed with no sign of Nick, she became convinced that he had indeed found someone to give him solitude without loneliness, a cipher like all his other women, herself included, but also a human presence in the emptiness, a living proof that he himself was alive, because he needed someone to fill the silent void created by his own hollowness and to remind him that he did in fact possess an identity as he made the difficult transition from Nick Rosney, committed media-man, back to Nick Rosney, so emotionally indigent that he was bored by everything, but above all by himself.

Even five years ago, Belle had subconsciously recognised the pain of the metamorphosis he underwent so often, but then she had been unable to suppress her resentment of the unpredictable touchiness it lent to him, as desperately in need of proofs of his love as he had been in need of peace and tolerant company in which to reconcile himself to the return to hollowness. Now, she was aware, quite consciously, of how she had failed him, and not even the fact that, unloving, he had deserved little better of her could stifle her regret.

If she could have made some atonement now, she would want to—but she would still be desperately afraid of the harm to herself, because nothing had changed. Nick still didn't love her and she was still sufficiently weak and human to wish that he did, and resent the denial of that wish.

The party looked like being an all-night affair and by three o'clock, still sober herself if a little light-headed, Belle was wondering whether to leave or see it out with the determined razzlers. She enjoyed this sort of gathering occasionally and was fortunate in rarely experiencing morning-after-effects since she had learnt the art of making drinks last a very long time and being careful never, ever, to mix them, but she was feeling depressed and weepy tonight, and obviously Nick wasn't going to put in an appearance now, she decided, becoming consumed with jealousy of whoever he had chosen to keep him company.

A number of her colleagues had departed already, but the majority remained, in varying stages of sobriety, or drunkenness, depending on one's viewpoint. The hard core were still deep in their favourite pastime of expounding on politics, everyone talking and no one listening, others were at the amorous or childish stages, and still others, men, were engaging in macho contests of skill or strength, arm-wrestling being the inevitable favourite, although there was a rather pointless drinking competition going on between two reporters who were down-downing their drinks and gradually turning green.

'Why do we do it, Marilyn?' Belle asked rather helplessly. 'If my mother could see some of these lunatic characters!'

'I know!' Marilyn laughed, watching Terry who was talking a mile a minute. 'It all gets so silly and rather sordid, doesn't it?'

'And we'd miss it like crazy if we lost it,' Belle realised. 'Even these affairs. I keep remembering that, on the job, most of these idiots are responsible, intelligent people, somewhat cynical but inherently kind. Is it dragons that have a soft spot? A soft underbelly? Or sharks?'

'You're rambling.'

'I'm still sober, though,' Belle laughed. 'Alert, lucid, focusing.'

'Are you, though? Your dynamic ex has just walked in and immediately become the cynosure of all eyes except yours. And you're the one who is hung up on him,' Marilyn teased, but her look was sympathetic as Belle suddenly lost all colour.

'Oh, God.'

Her heart was pounding, her pulses racing, and she knew that most of her sudden fear was for Nick. Even after such a short trip, Nick couldn't handle this sort of gathering. Not so soon.

But she was also afraid for herself. She didn't want to get involved again, but if she was the only person here who realised that he needed rescuing ...

She didn't think he had even noticed her. He was surrounded, and for a while Belle stayed as she was, a slender figure in a casual cream dress, leaning against the wall, glass in hand, apparently relaxed.

Her green eyes were observant, however, and she felt as if a hand were squeezing her heart, squeezing until she wanted to run from the pain of it. She remembered that look of Nick's, burnt-out and irritable. Nick-like, however, he was concealing the truth from all save her and Graham Thurlow, his smiles brilliant. Too brilliant, she thought, and he had downed his first drink at a gulp, probably on top of at least a couple on the flight back to Taipei.

Belle could hear as well as watch him because Nick Rosney was a man for whom others hushed. He was being funny, cracking ostensibly superficial jokes and making them laugh appreciatively, but she detected the blistering undertone to his wit and saw the stormy, warning flash of his vivid eyes if someone said something a little too slow or naïve.

Briefly, her eyes sought Graham Thurlow's and read their urgent message. She straightened, handing her glass to the now puzzled Marilyn.

'I've got to get him out of here,' she muttered.

For all their sakes, but Nick's most of all, and it was one way of atoning for her many failures five years ago. Too highly strung, he was in a dangerously temperamental mood just now.

Nevertheless, she had to steel herself to do what must be done, because it was all too likely that Nick's simmering wrath would boil over on to her when she intervened.

'Excuse me, please.' Her smile was bright and trivial as she steered a course through the throng surrounding Nick who stood flanked by Carey Devane and Deborah Palmer, hating each other and then looking startled by Belle's intervention. 'Sorry to break it up, but I rather urgently require a word with my ... husband. Nick?'

'Give her five minutes, Nick,' Graham backed her up. 'She deserves it.'

'Of course,' Nick conceded smoothly, his scintillating smile embracing everyone. 'For old times' sake. Excuse me, please.'

The hand he gave to Belle was burning but dry, as if he had a fever. She led him to the outer perimeter of the room, close to the door, heedless of the curious or resentful looks they drew, and turned so that he could stand with his back to the revellers, who quickly but reluctantly started other conversations with each other, resumed drinking or generally reverted to whatever they had been doing before Nick Rosney's arrival.

She looked up at him. His intensely deep blue eyes blazed in the shadowed sockets and his mouth had stopped smiling, its curve banished into a taut harsh line of strain.

'Was it bad, Nick?' she asked quietly.

That mouth moved, twisted. 'You never asked that before.'

'Better late,' she suggested lightly, feeling the sting of tears behind her eyes, and the knife of guilt in her heart and stomach. 'I'm asking now.'

'Oh, God.' He placed a hand on her shoulder and she felt some of his weight on her, and bore it for the first time. 'In a way, you cannot blame them. They're a poor country, the camps are full to overflowing and a crippling burden on the already strained economy, while other wealthier nations around the world sit back and are scandalised, but contribute nothing. But . . . There were children being sent back, Belle, and geriatrics, and a pregnant woman.'

'And men. They're just as vulnerable.' Belle laid a hand on his shoulder and ran it down the length of his arm, letting her fingers come to rest lightly over his wrist and hand. 'You don't have to stay here, you know, Nick.'

'I know, but——' He smiled crookedly.

'You don't want to be alone,' she supplied. 'Will I do? For company?'

His eyes went oddly blank. 'Oh, yes,' he said slowly. 'You'll do, Belle, you'll do.'

Anyone would do, she realised, and he didn't have to ask her because she was offering.

'Then——'

'Only . . .' Nick sounded resigned. 'I'm still too . . . wound up, or high, or something, to sleep tonight—this morning—and anyway, I'd never be free of interruptions at the hotel, even with the Do Not Disturb notice up. Everyone here and in London knows where I am.'

Belle hesitated only briefly. 'Can Deborah carry on for a day or so?'

'Yes.'

She looked at him consideringly. 'Then . . . Have you, as usual, unlimited funds?' She smiled faintly as he nodded. 'Then will you put yourself in my hands, Nick? I know somewhere we can go, a very short flight by jet, where you'll be left to do as you please.'

'I'm all yours, Belle.' He sounded serious, but being Nick, he had to follow it with a quick forced smile. 'It will be a novel experience, being taken charge of.'

She looked back at him, her lips quirking. 'Stop acting, Nick,' she said quietly. 'Shall we go? We both need to pack a few things, and I have a couple of 'phone calls to make.'

'What about your work, Belle?' Nick didn't move.

'That's one of the calls. Sue-Ching will appreciate the experience.'

'Ah, yes. A pretty girl.'

Belle couldn't contain her smile and their hands became linked in a clasp that tightened convulsively.

'Still crazy after all these years,' she laughed gently.

'Come on, move you! The night is nearly over and we have a plane to catch.'

The day was still young but already hot when they arrived in Hualien and checked into a coastal hotel overlooking a deserted beach washed by the Pacific.

Nick had grown quiet during the brief flight with East Asian Airlines, gradually realising that at last nothing was expected of him, but when Belle suggested on arrival that he might like to sleep, he had come to life, demanding that she show him why she had claimed that this region held a marvel that rivalled any of the more famous wonders of the world.

So they hired a car and Belle took the wheel.

Taroko Gorge with its thirty-eight tunnels, including the Swallow's Grotto where those birds flitted in and out, dipping and diving, gracefully swooping, was stupendously spectacular.

Mountains of pure marble towered above them, pagodas and shrines perched high and seemingly inaccessible on the heights. Waterfalls, foaming cascades of white lace, silvered by the sun, fell from on high; clear streams cut a way through the marble canyons far below the tortuously winding road.

It was a peaceful place, not deserted because such a miracle must always be attended by the beauty-loving human race, but no one bothered them, no one spoke to them, because no one was here for any reason save to worship Nature's work. Often they parked the car, to stroll through long, twisting tunnels with windows in the marble walls from which they could look down into water-filled ravines far, far below; to walk across the marble bridge of Motherly Devotion; or to climb to an exquisitely wrought, colourful pagoda with no sound to disturb them save the humming of bees.

This was Taiwan's principle marble-producing

region and an area where the aborigine culture was still strong in pockets, tribal customs still remembered.

They lunched high in the mountains, a simple Chinese meal at an unpretentious establishment which had never needed to produce anything more sophisticated because all food seemed prosaic to those who had just travelled through the grandeur of Taroko Gorge.

'Clever Belle, to think of it,' Nick murmured lethargically as they started the return drive. 'Perhaps this is what I need . . . every time. Or perhaps it's you. I missed the old Belle, but in some ways I prefer the new one.'

'I'm still the same Belle,' she returned expressionlessly.

He laughed, a little self-consciously she thought, probably because he thought he had sounded sentimental.

'I know, don't worry.' His tone altered abruptly. 'I suppose I'll have to bring the team here to get some footage of this miraculous magnificence.'

'Yes, you couldn't keep it to yourself, could you?' Belle challenged mischievously. She herself had been here twice before, but today meant so much more because she was sharing it.

'No,' Nick admitted. 'And old Graham deserves something like this after all the carnage and ugly heads of state he has had to shoot over the years.'

'And you deserve something like this to comment on,' she ventured, stirred by the weary, disillusioned tenor of his voice.

'I couldn't do it justice,' he disclaimed quietly. 'I think we'll have it silent, let it speak for itself.'

He eased himself into a more comfortable position and stayed quiet for so long that Belle thought he must have drifted into sleep, but when she stole a glance at

him, she realised that he had been overtaken by one of
the dark, silent moods that had once filled her with
both trepidation and resentment.

Now she knew better. The only thing she had to
fear where Nick was concerned was that he might
realise she still loved him and feel sorry for her, and
that was a discovery he was unlikely to make unless he
attempted to make love to her—which made her quite
safe for the present because he hadn't changed. The
pitifully little sexual appeal she had held for him had
failed her altogether when he was in this brooding,
introspective mood, suffering the agonies of withdrawal symptoms after the strange, angry highs he
experienced while engaged in his true work, attending
the appalling, the pitiful, the ugly aspects of reality,
where the trivia and niceties of ordinary everyday life
were eliminated by suffering and urgency. At these
times, with part of himself still left behind in whatever
hell he had been in and struggling to return, Nick was
incapable of politely pretending to want her.

As for her other fear, that any sort of involvement
with Nick would result in her being hurt, she had lost
it sometime between last night and this afternoon,
accepting that the mere fact of loving him made pain
inevitable.   The degree of it didn't matter.

On their return to their hotel, Nick disappeared
almost at once without a word of explanation and Belle
wondered if he now felt ready to sleep, but he rejoined
her a little later when she had changed into pale olive-
green shorts and a soft matching sleeveless T-shirt and
was sitting over an iced coffee in one of the hotel's
upstairs restaurants.

'The beach?' he enquired, glancing at her shorts as
he sat down.

'I was thinking of it, yes. I like to walk,' she said
cautiously.

'I'll join you then, if I may?' he said, waving a waitress away.

'Of course.' She studied his taut face for a few seconds. 'I thought you might have gone to sleep.'

'I'm not ready yet,' he responded abruptly. 'But you, Belle? You must be tired yourself. You were up all night.'

She shook her head. 'I don't need a lot of sleep.'

Her job had taught her not to need regular hours either, but in fact she was presently in that light-headed stage of fatigue, buoyed up by an excess of false energy that made her feel capable of running marathons or scaling mountains.

Nick looked at her appraisingly. 'You look tired . . . Why are you doing this, Belle?' he added very quietly.

Belle averted her face as a delicate flush coloured her cheeks. 'I don't know,' she lied, trying to sound nonchalantly amused.

He sighed. 'I don't know either, but I . . . appreciate it. You're supplying—what I need.'

She lifted her gaze, regret deepening the shadows lying in the depths of her constantly changing green eyes. 'I'm glad, and I hope that it may, in some small way, serve as . . . as compensation for all the times I failed to . . . supply, when we were married,' she told him slightly unsteadily, her remorse very evident.

Nick looked surprised, then annoyed and finally indifferent. 'Don't feel guilty about that, Belle. I never really expected anything else of you at the time . . . A child-bride, out of your depth.'

And of course, she reflected bleakly, her lack of understanding hadn't hurt him; it had merely irritated him, and contrition and forgiveness hardly arose in such a superficial context. She was the one who had been hurt, but by her own blind stupidity, she now realised. He had married her on a selfish impulse, it was true, but she had lacked the wit to detect it, her interpretation of his proposal so romantically rose-coloured that she could still squirm for her naïveté today.

During their walk on the beach and later, over drinks and dinner, Belle was forced to realise anew that her identity was a matter of indifference to Nick. She had no personality for him. Quite simply, all he required was peaceable companionship, someone to be an audience and make the right responsive noises if he decided to talk, and someone simply to be there if he was silent. Anyone would have done.

His mood seemed to grow darker and she was unsurprised when he excused himself immediately after concluding playing with his meal. Belle, however, lingered, ordering herself cassata and coffee. Hotel bedrooms were boring places, but foyers, restaurants, bars and lounges were full of fascinating fuel for the mind. She loved to stare at people, speculate about them and eavesdrop a little, since conversations conducted in public places could rarely be sacred and, anyway, she was a reporter and her father's daughter, born with a need to know.

So she sat and watched the world go by, in between thinking about Nick. As well as Chinese guests, the hotel catered for an international clientele, with a preponderance of Japanese and Australians, although Indians and Americans were also well-represented, and Belle watched them all and made guesses about them and wondered how many of their smiling faces hid pain and unhappiness such as she was feeling.

A sexy young Filipino in a John Travolta suit tried to pick her up and stayed to tell her his life story and answer her questions about his country. Belle sat and listened, forcing herself to pay attention and wondering if she should move on to the uncertainties of Manila next, since Taiwan looked likely to become a place of unhappy memories.

Finally, she excused herself, refusing his eager offer to escort her, and went to her room which was next door to Nick's. She put through a call to Sue-Ching in Taipei, who assured her that she had coped adequately and that no problems or sensational new stories had arisen.

'Everyone here is talking about you and Nick Rosney, Belle,' she added with a giggle. 'About the way you both simply disappeared. Miss Palmer and Miss Devane have both been in to interrogate me, but I told them nothing, nothing at all. I couldn't, anyway, because you yourself told me nothing.'

Belle experienced a wryly amused sense of satisfaction at the idea of Deborah and Carey being jealous of her for a change. She could guess what they would be thinking and it rather pleased her. They weren't to know that Nick's need of her at this time was purely asexual.

She bathed and prepared for bed, picturing Nick asleep at last next door, but as she sat at her dressing-table brushing her hair, she registered the faint, restless sounds that came from the next room.

She got up and moved slowly towards the bed, pausing thoughtfully in the middle of the room.

No, she decided, she couldn't carry it that far.

She lay down, switching out the light, but almost immediately she sat up again. In darkness she moved to the balcony door and opened it, stepping out and leaning over the railing as far as she could without losing her balance, turning her gaze in the direction of Nick's room.

His light was on, she saw, and then, quite clearly, she heard him swear in a weary, exasperated fashion.

Belle went inside again, still thoughtful. She could

come to no harm, she supposed; there could be no self-betrayal because Nick wouldn't want to make love to her. He never had at these times, although he had once assured her that he was fully capable of it but had simply chosen not to make love to her.

And he wouldn't choose to do so now, either, she knew. Nothing had changed.

Nevertheless, she hesitated, with a feeling of precognition, as if she stood on the verge of something cataclysmic and, if once the first step was taken, there could be no going back.

A wildly fanciful idea, she dismissed it. She wasn't given to presentiment. It was merely fatigue making her light-headed and causing her mind to leap about like this, nervous and knowing . . . a delusion.

Anyway, Nick needed her. Or rather, he needed someone, anyone. She mustn't forget that. It was an impersonal requirement, a need simply for any living human being, she supposed.

Belle drew on her slim-fitting robe, creamy-white satin with a scattered pattern of golden freesias, and slipped her room key into the pocket.

Then she went next door.

CHAPTER TEN

NICK looked at Belle rather blankly on opening the door in response to her knock, almost as if he didn't recognise her, she thought with slight hysteria.

She remembered that look so well. It had always had the power to wound her because it meant she was no longer getting through to him; he had switched off.

'What's wrong?' she asked dispassionately. 'Why can't you sleep?'

Nick gave a short angry laugh. 'Would you believe, because I'm too tired! I'm too bloody tired to sleep.'

He sat down on the edge of his rumpled bed and put his face in his hands. Belle stared at him. So rarely had she been permitted to witness his vulnerable human moments, and the sight disturbed her. Equally disturbing, but in an altogether different way, was the knowledge that beneath his thin short robe, he was naked. She could visualise the lean brown length of him, the strength . . .

Swiftly she suppressed that trend of thought, knowing it would hamper her in what she had to do. Her importunings and feeble attempts at seduction weren't what Nick needed.

Glancing at the air-conditioning control switch to make sure the room couldn't be any cooler, she went over to him.

'Nick?' Her voice sounded faint and nervous, a tiny sound. 'Nick, if we did as we used to when you were tired like this? Do you remember? You used to want to just . . . hold me, and then you'd go to sleep like that? Would it help?'

He looked up at her suspiciously, but after a few moments she saw an exhausted resignation come into his eyes. His mouth twisted derisively.

'We could try it,' he conceded drily.

Belle moved uncertainly. 'Shall I ... Let me straighten the bedclothes first, then.'

He moved to allow her access to the sheets.

'Do I keep this on?' He indicated his robe amusedly and she blushed.

'I think so, yes,' she said gravely, straightening up after completing her task.

He lay down, pulling up just the covering sheet, and she hesitated again, then slowly removed her own robe before slipping into bed beside him, carefully holding down the hem of her brief night-shirt, white with rich golden-yellow piping and short enough to reveal almost the entire length of her thighs.

She turned to Nick rather self-consciously and he switched out the light before drawing her into his arms, sighing as he did so.

'Dear God, what have I come to?' he laughed with a bitter self-mockery a few seconds later and Belle winced at the harsh sound. 'Here is my once adoring wife, feeling sorry for me! Times have changed rather drastically.'

'Don't talk,' she advised through clenched teeth, and he was obediently silent.

Too tired, he had said, but it seemed more likely that he was too tense to sleep, she realised. Every muscle was knotted with tension and he was holding himself absolutely rigid. He was hot too, burning hot, and she wondered if his weariness was being exacerbated by some sort of fever.

She was careful to lie very still, remembering how any movement had irritated him in the old days, but it was even more difficult than she had expected. The old, familiar, sweet melting sensation had afflicted her the moment he touched her, and the fiery warmth of his body had transformed it into a molten heat that affected every part of her. Every nerve-end was sensitised, crying out for more than just his arms about her, wanting caresses, kisses, his full possession; her very pores were dilated in responsive awareness of his nearness and her blood flowed close to the surface of her skin so that she felt as if a deep burning flush covered not only her face but her entire body.

And she must be still . . .

To her surprise, it was Nick who was stirring, restless, fretful movements, slightly jerky as if he strove to contain them.

'Nick?' She realised that he was trembling.

'Ah, no! I can't!' His protest emerged as an agonised groan as he pushed her away. 'It's no good, this isn't going to work, Belle . . . It has been too long! Go away, quickly, go back to your room. Please! I shouldn't have yielded to the temptation to hold you in my arms.'

'But, Nick, what . . .'

'God help me, I can't let you go!' His arms closed round her again, convulsively. 'I can't stop myself, I can't help myself! I must, I've got to . . . Let me . . . It has been so long. I want you, I want you!'

Shocked, Belle realised that he was fully aroused, swollen with his need of her. Still muttering feverishly, Nick shuddered violently as she slid her arms about him, lifting her face in the darkness. She didn't know what it was all about, and she wasn't asking. She only knew that at long last, Nick wanted her in the way she had always dreamed of, the way she wanted him, urgently and consumingly, with a hot, violent hunger.

That hunger seemed to explode in the meeting of

their mouths and they were swept into a whirling, swirling kaleidoscope of passion. When the kiss ended, Nick tore off his robe and Belle sat up to pull off her night-shirt.

Then they fell on each other, in a fierce frenzy of mutual need, as if they would devour each other. Nick was gasping even as she was, and Belle felt her heart and mind expanding to contain the joy that flooded them like a brilliant light. At last, after all these years, she was being freed to respond to him with the entirety of her love and passion because Nick, too, was wildly out of control, all restraint abandoned as he swept her into the maelstrom of his furious passion.

How it had happened, she didn't understand, but she knew without needing to analyse it or even think about it that this time Nick's involvement equalled hers. He was here with her, all the way, with every part of himself.

His hands and mouth were at every part of her body, sweeping over her burning flesh, hurting her slightly with the ferocity of his passion, but Belle could only delight in such evidence of his desire, just as she delighted in the harsh groans she drew from him with her own feverish caresses.

'Never, Belle!' Nick was talking incoherently, his breathing ragged. 'Not this way . . . Never, ever! I swore it, Belle! And now . . .'

'It's all right.'

She didn't know what he meant, but he sounded so tortured that she had to offer the reassurance.

They moved together with mounting urgency, the wanting becoming concentrated, and intolerable. Nick dragged rasping, tortured breaths into his lungs and Belle heard her own husky moans as desire leapt to become unbearable need.

'Belle!' Nick sounded anguished.

'It's all right, Nick,' she sobbed, opening to him, arching. 'Don't wait! Now, Nick . . . please!'

She heard the sharp sound he made at the moment of penetration, mingling with her own hoarse throbbing cry. His possession of her was deep and violent, hurting her, but there was also a rapture such as she had never known before, so incredible, so complete, that she thought she was dying.

Her fingers raked his shoulders, her cries filled the room as she responded to the fierce thrusting of his body, and a wild joy flooded her because at last Nick was going with her all the way, loving and loved, possessing and possessed because not only was his body contained in hers, joining them, but also his mind and his heart and even his soul became part of her, making them truly one.

'Belle!' he cried her name as they were convulsed together, at the pinnacle of a searing ecstasy so exquisite, so perfect, that Belle almost lost consciousness, clinging violently to Nick with a wild, shuddering cry as multiple waves of unutterable pleasure spasmed through her, reaching every part of her body and filling her mind with a brilliant white light, before they toppled down together into warm, soft darkness, floating, drifting and slowly spinning back to mortality after their matchless experience of the divine.

Spent, Nick collapsed against Belle, sleeping almost immediately. For a time, she lay awake, stroking the dark head that lay against her breasts, smiling tenderly in the darkness, utterly content. Her lips were bruised, her breasts tender from the primitive passion of his kisses and handling, and there was a slight ache in her lower back, but at the same time she knew a euphoric sense of wellbeing such as she had never experienced before.

She had no thoughts, no questions for the moment, only knowledge, a knowledge so sure and gloriously perfect that she fell asleep soon afterwards, more happily than she had ever done in her life.

She woke before Nick. He had moved during the night and now lay turned towards her, one hand resting on the curve of her waist.

The sweet pale morning light revealed their lower limbs entangled in the sheets and Belle smiled to herself, remembering the way it had been. She lay watching him sleep with loving eyes, waiting for him to wake.

He looked better already, she reflected, yesterday's harsh lines smoothed out, some of the weary tautness gone, and the shadows of fatigue were fewer, the pallor less, so that his tan was evident once more.

The hand at her waist stirred, fingers tightening and then relaxing again, and Nick opened his eyes. Belle smiled radiantly at him and he smiled faintly in return, but a moment later she saw appalled recollection enter his eyes and he snatched his hand away from her waist. He closed his eyes briefly and when he opened them again, his look was wary, guarded.

Belle's faint sigh contained compassion as she understood, but she had no intention of losing what she had found.

'What was it all about, Nick?' she asked lightly.

The vivid eyes went blank—studiously blank, she realised. Then he gave her one of his quick, meaningless smiles.

'Bad timing,' he suggested flippantly. 'I gather I . . . lost control, somewhat.'

'Don't try to laugh it off, you buttoned-up idiot. I'm serious, I want to know,' she told him, still keeping her tone light. 'You surprised me last night. How long has this been going on?'

He gave her a hunted look, almost despairing, before turning on to his back and staring at the ceiling. He laughed a little, an uncertain sound.

'Since the moment I first set eyes on you five and a half years ago,' he admitted, He glanced at her again. 'Crazy, isn't it? Belle!'

She hadn't been expecting that, having imagined that it had happened since his arrival in Taiwan, and she had gone chalk white, tears filling her suddenly shadowy eyes which moments before had been clear and full of light. She sat up agitatedly.

'Ah, no, Nick, tell me it's not true,' she begged in a piteous whisper, her lips trembling. 'I can't have failed you to that extent . . . Ah, God, you must have been so disappointed in me, so . . .'

He touched her shoulder quickly. 'You never failed me, dearest girl. I wasn't that stupid. I knew I couldn't expect anything more from an infatuated eighteen-year-old. I had only myself to blame for . . . for everything, because I was always aware that I shouldn't have married you. It was taking unfair advantage of your infatuation. I tried to resist the temptation, but I knew, the way you were, that you'd probably accept any proposal of mine and . . . I think I went a little crazy at the time. I had to have something of you before it wore off, and I thought it might last a little longer if we were married instead of merely lovers. You outgrew it so quickly, didn't you? That first time, our wedding night, was the only time you really enjoyed my lovemaking. Once you'd had it all, knew it all . . . I wasn't surprised, though, and certainly it was no failure on your part. I bought my own hell when I gave in to my . . . my obsession, instead of fighting it. And it was hell, I might as well admit that, now that you know what a fool I am. The worst was not being able to make love to you the way I wanted to. I had to be so careful, and I used to ache to show you the way I really felt. I could never stay in the bed with you after we'd been together ... And now you know why I never made love to you immediately after my returns from my assignments. I knew my self-control was weakened during those periods, as you discovered last night, and I had to wait until I could be sure of it again.'

Belle sank back against the pillows, staring at his drawn face, and a tear slid down her cheek as she began to comprehend the needlessness of the barren, wasted years behind.

'But why?' she asked brokenly. 'Why did you have to ... to be controlled, Nick? Why couldn't you show me how you felt, in bed if in no other way?'

She was surprised to see him flush slightly.. 'For one thing, because I was terrified of making a fool of myself—as I did last night,' he admitted abruptly. 'After that first time, you were always so reserved. I was constantly aware of a certain restraint and I realised that while you could handle and even enjoy that sort of polite, gentle sex, anything more would probably have frightened you away; you'd have felt pressurised, that I was making demands it was beyond your capacity to fulfil ... So I was always very careful. I was terrified that if you discovered the extent of my ... obsession, it would oppress you and you'd leave even sooner than you had to anyway. I always knew I had to lose you. Infatuation couldn't last and I spent most of our marriage expecting you to announce your departure. I was desperate, but I knew there was no way I could hold you once you'd cast off the last remnants of your infatuation and stopped idolising me ... I had to let you go, or you'd have learnt to hate me, resent me, When you did go . . . Ah, God, I can't describe the last five years, missing you, wanting you, and knowing I had no right to seek you. I tried to forget you by being with other women, but I found myself resenting them because they weren't you. When you started supplying material for actuality radio programmes, I tuned in whenever I was in a place where they carried your reports, just to hear your voice. When I knew I was going to see you again, I . . . I don't know what I thought and felt, but I think I knew I'd try to make love to you again. Only, I didn't intend it to be last night, and certainly not that way, Belle.'

'Oh, Nick,' she choked, laying a hand along his hard cheek, and he flinched.

'Don't! Don't feel sorry for me, I can't bear it!'

'I feel sorry for both of us,' she said sadly, smoothing back the black hair that fell over his brow. 'Because my own story is so ironically similar. But where did you get the idea that it was infatuation, Nick . . . Nick, my love? I can say the words. Can't you? I love you, I've loved you from the moment we met and I've never stopped loving you.'

A distressing spasm of anguish passed over his face. 'Then—why?' he groaned, the words wrung from him.

The look in his eyes stirred her, a compound of despair and desperate hope.

'It seems I understood you better before we got married than I have ever done since,' she confessed regretfully. 'I knew why you asked me to marry you, Nick . . . But then I lost sight of it. It didn't seem to be the real reason any more. Your reserve, your restraint, made me learn to be that way too because it seemed, if I responded to you as I wanted to, that I'd be the one making a fool of myself and I'd have hated you to pity me. And I never told you either because

... you seemed to want to keep it casual, and if ever I did become emotional, you were irritated.'

'Because when you did, it always seemed to be in a way that confirmed the growth of your disillusionment and I hated the knowledge that I was losing you,' he inserted painfully.

'I was looking for proofs, I think,' Belle admitted sorrowfully. 'And when I realised you had been waiting for me to leave ... Oh, Nick, it just seemed to confirm what I'd grown to believe, that you'd married me because you were bored, to amuse yourself by shocking your friends. You once said it was an impulse, marrying me.'

'I suppose it was in a way, because I hadn't meant to yield to ... to my ...'

'Obsession,' she supplied with a wry tenderness, her smile ruefully indulgent.

He flushed slightly. 'Yes. I had meant to resist it but, dear God, Belle, I couldn't handle it. I couldn't believe what had happened to me, instantly. There had never been anything like it ... I was a little mad, I think. All I could think of was that I had to have something of you, for a time at least, just whatever you could give me for as long as you could.'

'And I could have given so much more than I did,' she reminded him achingly, her eyes full of shame. 'If only I'd known ... no, if only I hadn't stopped remembering why you married me. Because I did know once, only later I thought I'd deceived myself ... I feel awful about it, Nick, and I'm so sorry, so sorry ...'

'Stop blaming yourself!' He drew her close because she was weeping with a poignant regret for the pointless waste that lay behind them, the needless suffering. 'You were eighteen and inevitably a little unsure of yourself. You needed more reassurance than

I gave you . . . I gave you very little altogether, didn't I? But you see, I didn't know, Belle, I didn't know you . . . loved me.'

'And now, Nick?' She looked up at him.

'And now?' He returned her look with a reluctant supplication and the question seemed to be dragged from him. 'Do we have a second chance, Belle? Please?'

'Oh, yes, we're that lucky,' she breathed. 'Do you mean marriage, though, Nick?'

'Yes,' he assured her curtly. Then he laughed. 'God! I rushed into divorce the same way I rushed into marriage, so we'll have to do it all over again, won't we?'

'Well, we can dispense with the big ceremony this time, I think,' she offered, smiling.

'We have a problem with our careers, though.' His eyes had grown rather bleak now. 'And I don't want it to be the way it was before, either. I hated leaving you, I seemed to need you more than ever when I was away, and the absences made the returns equally hard.'

'Can I tell you one of my favourite fantasies?' Belle requested shyly. 'I've thought that you might let me accompany you, Nick, when it was possible and where it was allowed. I could be a sort of roving reporter. My clients would probably complain initially about the change, but as I'm a freelance contributor they can't prevent it and I hardly think they'd stop using my reports if I was filing on the same events you cover. Those are the really big news, the action stories, aren't they?'

'It could work,' Nick said slowly. 'But they're bad scenes, some of them, Belle.'

'I know. We'd help each other to keep sane. Of course, if there was a baby . . .' She stopped, struck by a possibility. 'You do realise that you could already have made me pregnant, Nick? I wasn't—protected.'

'Would you mind?' he asked cautiously, eyes blank, and Belle realised they still had a way to go before he was truly free of his inhibitions.

'I want your baby, darling,' she assured him quietly and felt him relax.

'We'd both have to modify our careers if there was one. But I thought you were a committed career woman?' he teased.

'Well, men with careers never mind having families,' she pointed out mischievously.

'It's somewhat different for a woman,' he said drily.

'Is it?' Belle asked innocently, eyes glimmering with laughter. 'The conception at any rate seems to affect men and women in pretty much the same way . . . But we'll cross that bridge if and when we come to it, Nick. If we go on trusting and believing in each other, it shouldn't present a problem . . . But I want you to know that I want your child for the right reasons this time . . . And in a way, it was always my reason.'

'God!' Nick's face darkened as he remembered. 'If you knew what it did to me that time, Belle, hearing you ask me to give you a baby . . . The idea of you, with my child . . . It was suddenly something I wanted more than anything in the world and I was so tempted to agree. It would have been a way of binding you to me . . . But I couldn't do that to you, trap you like that.'

'You could have bound me to you more easily than that,' she ventured gently. 'Three little words, Nick.'

'I know.' He spoke stiltedly, watching her through the screen of his long eyelashes. 'It was all mostly my fault, wasn't it? This stupid inability of mine . . . I wasn't able to reassure you, tell you . . .'

'You still can't say it, can you?'

Nick stirred restlessly, his expression dark and unhappy. 'It's this block I have . . .' he began.

'What makes it so difficult?' Belle asked softly. 'You've said it once to someone, haven't you? Long ago.'

'I don't recall.'

'I've met them, Nick, remember?'

She left it there, sensing his withdrawal—his retreat—and knowing that she was probing painful but long buried memories. Recently he had told her part of it, and one day he would tell her the rest, she thought, when his faith in her, in love, was complete, but this wasn't the time. It wasn't important.

'Does it mean so much to you?' he asked stiffly. 'I don't . . . I can't lose you again, Belle.'

'For myself, it doesn't matter. I know what I need to know—as I knew it when you asked me to marry you, only this time I won't forget it, I promise you,' she reassured him, kissing his throat and then tipping back her head to look into his tense face. 'No, I just thought you yourself might feel happier, free, if you could tell me.'

His lips moved, then tightened. 'I can't!' he protested tautly.

'But you can show me?' Smiling into his eyes, she ran a slender hand over him, fingers tangling in his body hair and finally coming to rest at the powerful line of his thighs, feeling him stir.

'Of course.' He was relieved, but his expression stayed serious. 'You're a merciful woman, Belle . . . Not to demand, when it was I . . . my . . . I'm sorry! Forgive me.'

'I have other demands to make,' she informed him mischievously, drawing one of his hands to her breasts and turning her mouth up to his.

'Which I will take pleasure in satisfying,' he laughed.

Belle knew he was steeling himself to restraint, to control. She had to accept that it could be a long time, months or even years, before he learnt sufficient trust to relax and reveal to her again the true depth of his feelings.

But she would never again make the mistake of trying to match him in reserve. She would never dissemble again. She had to tell him and show him the truth, over and over again, until she had instilled in him the complete confidence that would enable him to do the same.

So she let her own passionate emotions control her as Nick began to make love to her, crying aloud her love and desire as he brought her to hot pulsating life in an exquisite seduction of the senses, showing and telling him in every way possible just how deeply and devouringly she needed him.

She was swept along by a great tidal wave of passion, equally uninhibited in what she asked and what she gave, unashamed of the raw, erotic hunger his skilled sensuality created, knowing that beneath the constraint, he was experiencing the same thing.

There came a moment when she lay, panting shamelessly for release from the tension that had been building and building to an intolerable pitch, a fierce throbbing ache there in her loins where she wanted his strength, and as she looked up into Nick's taut dark face, she saw the startled wonder in his eyes as he beheld her frenzied arousal. She realised then that last night he had probably been too caught up in his own savage need to absorb the implications of her equal hunger and response.

'Belle!'

A great shudder racked his hard hot body and then,

as the shackles of restraint were cast aside, his lovemaking became compelling, frantic, a true expression of his feelings, exciting Belle beyond endurance, so that in being conquered, Nick became the conqueror, mastering her, dominant and demanding.

'Take me, Nick,' she begged harshly. 'Take me now, please!'

He possessed her strongly, deeply, commanding her compliance with the driving force of his impelling quest for satisfaction, and they beat upwards together to a rapture even more powerful than last night's because now he was as conscious of her love, her exquisite pleasure, as she of his.

And at the towering peak of their union, as Belle sobbed with ecstasy, locked in the last violent paroxysm of utter, perfect fulfilment, she heard Nick's voice.

'I love you!' The words were torn from his throat. 'I love you, Belle, I love you!'

A long time later she lifted a still trembling hand to the dampness of his dark hair.

'Nick, Nicky, Nick, my love,' she murmured, almost crooning the words, the refrain that had rung in her mind through all the years and could now be uttered aloud without fear of ridicule.

He lifted his head to smile at her, his mouth tender in a face that held peace at last, but laughter sparkled in his eyes.

'If you ever call me Nicky in public, I'll divorce you.'

'You'll have to marry me first,' she retorted.

'Yes. Ah, Belle!' He sobered, gently kissing her face and regarding her with loving eyes from which all reserve was gone. 'Do you know what you've done, you wonderful, miraculous woman? For the first time in my life, I feel whole, and healed . . .'

'I've done nothing except love you,' Belle said simply.

'And I love you.' Nick laughed suddenly. 'Do you realise what you've let yourself in for? You're going to have to keep on listening to it for the rest of your life. Now that you've got me started, I can't stop saying it ... I love you, I love you, I love you!'

'Keep on talking, Nick, I like the sound of that! Incidentally, how does it feel, coming out, you closet lover?'

They clung to each other, laughing for the sheer joy of knowing themselves free at last of the inhibitions that had silenced their long love for each other.

The loving had been begun long years ago and on the other side of the world. Now it was come to full and glorious maturity, perfected by the knowledge that it would have no conclusion.

Harlequin Presents

Coming Next Month

Available in October wherever paperback books are sold, or through Harlequin Reader Service:

In the U.S.
P.O. Box 1397
Buffalo, N.Y.
14240-1397

In Canada
P.O. Box 2800, Postal Station A
5170 Yonge Street
Willowdale, Ontario M2N 6J3

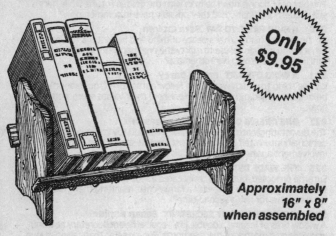

HARLEQUIN HISTORICAL

Explore love with Harlequin in the Middle Ages, the Renaissance, in the Regency, the Victorian and other eras.

Relive within these books the endless ages of romance, set against authentic historical backgrounds. Two new historical love stories published each month.

HIST-A-1

Could she find love as a mail-order bride?

MARIANNE WILLMAN

PIECES OF SKY

In the Arizona of 1873, Nora O'Shea is caught between life with a contemptuous, arrogant husband and her desperate love for Roger LeBeau, half-breed Comanche Indian scout and secret freedom fighter.

———————◆————————

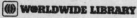